TALES FROM THAILAND

TALES FROM THAILAND
Fact and Fancy

by

LOTUS

Illustrated by
BEN KLOEZEMAN

M.P.H. PUBLICATIONS SDN. BHD.
SINGAPORE
1968

Printed by
M.P.H. PRINTERS SDN. BHD.
SINGAPORE
1968

FOREWORD

All these stories have been previously published either in the "Bangkok Post" or the "Weekly Illustrated of India," or both, except "Golden Eye," which was published in the "Asia Magazine."

I have in some stories used the word "Thailand," and in others "Siam." This is because the stories have been written over a number of years, during which the name of the country has been officially changed several times. At the present time, the name in use is "Thailand," but many people are in favour of reverting to the name "Siam."

The race of people known as Thai comprise the inhabitants of the Kingdoms of Thailand and Laos, the Shan States in Burma and Southern China, and many smaller tribes in various parts of China.

The word "Lao" is generally use to denote an inhabitant of the Kingdom of Laos or Northern Thailand. There are also many Lao people in the Province of Khorat in Central Thailand.

The term "Siamese," strictly speaking, applies only to the people of Southern Thailand and the Thai Peninsular Provinces.

Some of the stories in this book are founded on fact, some have been told to me as true by Thai friends, some I have invented.

Among the true stories are "Lamyai Girl," "The Ferryman," "The Gangster," and "Blackmail." Stories told me as true include;— "The Third Rider," "Feeding the Fishes," and "The Two Corporals."

But in my heart, I feel that all my stories are true. Anyhow, whether they be good or bad, I believe that I am the only man who could have written them. Few, if any, "farangs" have lived in the country for sixty-six years, as I have done; few, if any, know the Thai people so well as I do, and I am quite certain that none love the country and people so dearly.

Lotus.

Chiengmai, Thailand,
January, 1962.

v

CONTENTS

GLOSSARY

TITLES

Phya.	Thai title of nobility.
Luang.	Thai title of nobility.
Towkay.	Form of address to Chinese merchant.
Chao.	Prince or Chief
Muen.	Minor title conferred by Northern Chiefs
Saen.	Minor title conferred by Northern Chiefs.
Nan.	Prefix used by an ex-monk.
Noi.	Prefix used by an ex-novice.
Nai.	Master or Mr.
Nang.	Mrs. In former times used also to means Miss.
Nangsao.	Miss.
Ai.	Prefix for a man who has never been ordained. In South Thailand this is a derogatory term
Sang.	Prefix used by a Shan ex-monk.
Chao Khun.	Your Excellency. His Excellency.
Pu.	Grandfather.
Yai.	Grandmother.
Lung.	Uncle.
Kamnan.	Village Headman.

MONEY

Baht.	Thai monetary unit. Pre-war value 1s/11d. Present value 4d. approx.
Stang.	Cent. 100th part of baht.
Att.	64th part of Baht. Obsolete since 1910.
Salung.	Quarter of baht.
Fuang.	Eighth of baht.
Taep.	Rupee. Formerly current in North Thailand.

Nai Hang.	Manager of a firm.
Muang.	Province or City.
Ban.	Village.
Lamut.	A fruit. Sapota.
Lamyai.	A fruit. Nephilim Longana.
Matayom.	Educational Standard.
Farang.	European or American.
Amphur.	Administrative District.
Nai Amphur.	District Officer.
Tiger.	Prefix used for a robber or notorious criminal.
Lao.	(as used in this book) An inhabitant of Northern Thailand.
Shan.	An inhabitant of the Shan States of Burma.
Samlor.	Tricycle.

GREEN LOTUS

"Please, Nai, will you advance me one month's pay. I am thinking of getting married."

Noi Parn always talked like that. Short and to the point. He was a surly sort of fellow, and nobody liked him. However, he was a pretty good cook.

"Whom do you intend to marry?" I asked.

"Miss Green Lotus, the girl next door," replied Noi Parn.

This rather suprised me. I knew the girl well by sight, and very pleasing she was to the eye; but I had supposed for some time past that there was a sort of understanding between her and my house-boy, Saen, a lively young blade, and a particular favourite of mine. However, it was none of my business.

So I gave Noi Parn the money he asked for, and a week or two later he was duly married to Green Lotus, and went to live with her at her parents' house next door, as is usual in Northern Siam.

It had not occurred to me that Saen would worry himself much about this. Indeed, I had no idea how far things might have gone between him and Green Lotus. I was, therefore, very surprised to notice that, from the time of Noi Parn's marriage, Saen's character seemed to change completely. He became dull and taciturn, neglected his work, and quarrelled with his fellow-servants. This went on for several months. Then I decided to have it out with Saen, so I called him up and asked him whether he was unhappy or dissatisfied. He broke down completely, started to weep, and said:- "Nai, I cannot go on working. I love Green Lotus, and she told me she loved me too, but her parents compelled her to marry Noi Parn, because his relations are richer than mine. His father owns a large rice-field and several buffaloes, while mine has nothing but a small vegetable garden. If she had been living somewhere far away, I could have borne it; but she lives close by, and I have to see her and Noi Parn together all the time. It upsets me, and makes me hate Noi Parn. If I stay here, some day I may do him an injury. So I have made up my mind to enter the priesthood. Let me go, Nai, and I will become a priest at the Suan Dawk temple, and stay there until my soul is at peace."

I was fond of Saen, and did not want to lose him; but I realised that his mind was very troubled, and felt that perhaps his plan of donning the yellow robe might be the best way to overcome his sorrow. So I agreed to let him go, and a couple of weeks later he became a priest at Wat Suan Dawk.

When Noi Parn and Green Lotus had been married for about nine months, a child was born to them — a girl. Not long after that, Noi Parn's father died suddenly, and his relations pressed him to enter the priesthood during the coming Lenten season, in order to acquire merit for his father's soul. This is very often done, and in the case of a married man, his wife's consent must be obtained, and he is forbidden to see her alone during his term in the temple.

Like Saen, Noi Parn was ordained at Wat Suan Dawk. So there were the two rivals, both priests in the same temple, sleeping in adjoining cells, and praying side by side several times a day. According to what I was later told by the Head Priest, nobody in the temple supposed that there was any ill feeling between them.

When Noi Parn had been a priest for about two months, I was sitting one morning at breakfast, when one of my servants rushed in, shouting:- "Nai, Nai, Saen has hacked Noi Parn to death with a sword, and has been taken to the lock-up in the Police Station!"

It was true. Here is what happened, as revealed a month later, when Saen was put on his trial for murder.

Early that morning, Saen, or Phra Saen, as he was then called, woke up early and came out of his cell; the first thing he saw was a paper, nailed to the door of the cell; and this is what was written on it:-

"The priest who occupies this cell has broken the most holy laws of the priesthood. He goes outside the temple walls at night to meet an evil woman."

On reading this, Saen was filled with fury. At the same

2

moment he saw Noi Parn coming towards him. He tore the paper from the door, and showed it to Noi Parn.

"Did you write this?" he asked.

"Yes," answered Noi Parn, "I wrote it, and it is true. I saw you with my own eyes."

There was a party of Shan peddlers staying in the temple rest-house. One of them was selling swords, and his basket, containing several long Shan swords, was standing on the ground nearby. Saen ran to the basket, pulled out a sword, and struck Noi Parn with it four times on the face and neck. Noi Parn fell down. Saen continued frantically to hack at him as he lay on the ground, until the Shan traders dragged him away. But by that time, Parn was already dead.

When the Head Priest came hurrying up to see what all the commotion was about, Saen went and knelt at his feet, saying:- "I have committed murder. Do with me as you think best."

By this time the Police had been called in, and Saen, hurriedly stripped of his yellow robe, was haled away to the lock-up.

Now, had Saen been a layman, he would probably have escaped with a sentence of imprisonment. He had, no doubt, received grave provocation, as a serious charge which, if true, would have meant his ruin, had been brought against him. Moreover, he had acted on impulse, seizing the nearest weapon which came to his hand, before his anger had time to cool.

But poor Saen was a Buddhists priest. He had taken a solemn vow to refrain from taking the life even of an animal or an insect. It would have been a sin for him to crush a mosquito. By slaying a fellow man and a fellow priest he had committed a crime which struck at the very roots of Buddhist morality. No Siamese Court could possibly have passed on him any other sentence than one of death.

* * *

Saen sat on the ground, his hands tied behind his back, his eyes blindfolded, pellets of mud in his ears, to prevent him from hearing the executioners as they approached.

There were two executioners, both dressed in red, with scarlet flowers behind their ears. Both were more or less drunk — it would be difficult to get a Thai man to kill a fellow-creature unless he had a fair amount of liquor in him. They stood behind a small bush, whence they emerged two or three times waving their swords with theatrical gestures, evidently getting themselves worked up to the point of carrying out their horrible duty. Then the taller and more sober of the executioners, after several false alarms, suddenly sprang forward and dealt a tremendous blow at Saen's neck, severing the spinal column. The smaller man then finished off the work, carving the head from the body with his sword. When the bandage on the dead man's face had been removed, the head was elevated on a stake for all to see. As the stake entered his neck, Saen's eyes opened for a moment, and looked at me.

I have seen many dead men, but none of their faces bore such a look of calm and peace as that of the "murderer" whose head had just been violently struck from his body.

Feeling more dead than alive, I turned and went slowly home.

Green Lotus was kneeling in my verandah, holding her baby girl, and convulsed with weeping.

"I killed him, I killed him," she sobbed. "But for me, he would still be alive."

I tried to comfort her. "Sister," I said, "you are not to blame. You could not have saved him."

"I killed him," she repeated. "It was I who went to meet him outside the temple wall at night, and Parn saw us there, though he did not recognise me in the dark. I went there because Saen wanted so much to see my baby, and could not well go to my house in the daytime. I ought not to have gone."

"But, Sister," I said, "I do not understand. Why should he who is dead want to see Parn's baby?"

"Nai," she answered, "you knew him and you loved him. Look at my baby. Look into her eyes."

I took up the little child and looked intently into her eyes. Then I thought of the eyes which had looked at me less than an hour before from the calm, dead face of the "murderer" Saen.

And I understood.

Note. The events related in this story took place in the year
A.D. 1905.

4

THE ISLAND

The islands, in the rivers of Thailand come and go. When the rains cease in November, little islands appear. They are eagerly occupied by market gardeners and planted with vegetables. In June or July the little islands vanish, save for a few unusually solid ones, which last from year to year; but even these seemingly permanent islands may be swept away during a heavy flood.

The island known as Bullfrog Island had been in existence for at least thirty or forty years. It was separated from the river-bank by a channel about fifty feet wide. In the dry season, this channel was a mere ditch, by the end of the rains a swiftly flowing stream, in flood-time a raging torrent.

For four or five years two men owned vegetable gardens on Bullfrog Island. Uncle Nuan was a man of fifty, a widower, known to all the neighbours as the meanest man for miles around. He shared the island with Noi Larn, a jolly young bachelor of twenty-three. There was little love lost between the two men. Noi Larn called his neighbour "Uncle Tightfist" and the older man retaliated with "Master Wastrel." Both were good gardeners and did well with their vegetables, but while Uncle Nuan had saved a tidy sum, Noi Larn never had a cent left over, and had even borrowed a hundred bahts from his fellow-islander.

One September morning a few years ago, Uncle Nuan awoke to find the south end of the island under water. It was the beginning of the biggest flood within living memory. The waters were already lapping the walls of his hut. He hurried to rouse Noi Larn. After a look round, the two men decided that there was nothing to be done but abandon the island. The channel between them and the river-bank was by this time a roaring whirlpool of water which was rapidly rising. There was a rough bridge, made of two bamboos, across the channel, but it was clear that this would soon be carried away by the torrent.

Uncle Nuan was terrified. "Nothing can save me," he wailed, "I cannot swim, and I dare not cross that bamboo bridge. The handrail is broken, and I shall fall into the river and be drowned."

Noi Larn was not worried. He was a big, strong fellow, and a good swimmer. Though the rush of water was fierce, he felt quite capable of tackling a channel only fifty feet wide. However, he realised that his companion was in a tight spot, so he said:—

"Get onto my back, Uncle Tightfist, and I will carry you across the bridge. But you must stay perfectly still, or we shall both fall into the river."

The old man viewed with horror the prospect of being borne across a shaky bamboo bridge. But it was his only chance. So up he got onto Noi Larn's back. Then, slowly and gingerly, like Blondin crossing the rapids of Niagara, the young man bore his trembling companion across the raging stream.

When they reached the opposite bank, Uncle Nuan was profuse in his thanks. "My dear son Larn," he whimpered, "you have saved my life at the risk of your own. How can I ever reward you?"

"That's easy enough," replied Noi Larn. "Just let me off that hundred bahts I owe you, and we'll call it square."

Uncle Nuan's face fell. "You are asking too much," said he. "A hundred bahts is a lot of money. But I do not want to seem ungrateful. I will let you off ten bahts. Pay me back ninety bahts, and we will call it a deal."

"What!" cried the young man. "You mean old scoundrel. If you only value your life at ten bahts, it is not worth bothering to save it!"

Then, lifting Uncle Nuan in his arms, he cried:— "I am going to carry you back to the island. Stay still, or I will chuck you into the river."

Suiting the action to the words, he once more stepped upon the bamboo bridge and carried the miserable old fellow back to the island. At the moment when he set foot on land the bridge collapsed.

"Here we are, Uncle Tightfist," said Noi Larn. "Now you can shift for yourself. But I do not want to be in your debt. Take this ring. It is worth more than a hundred bahts. So I am paying my debt in full, plus interest."

6

Then he plunged into the channel, and in a few minutes was safe on the opposite bank.

Half an hour later Bullfrog Island had vanished completely beneath the waters of the flood. As for Uncle Tightfist, nobody ever knew what happened to him. But he got the gold ring, anyhow.

THE CLAMMY HAND

Travellers in Northern Thailand are generally glad to camp near a Buddhist temple — it is always clean there. The next best place is in the neighbourhood of a Police Station. So when, one afternoon in June, 1907, I arrived, on a journey from Nan to Prae, at the little village of Ban Puang, and found there an open green space, with a pretty little temple on one side and a miniature Police Station on the other, I quickly gave orders to unload my elephants, and set up camp there for the night.

The officer in charge of the Police Station proved to be an old friend from Prae, Lieutenant Sanit. He strolled across while I was having my tea, and I, by way of being polite, expressed satisfaction at the near presence of him and his men, in case any thieves or robbers might be hanging about the place.

"Do not worry about thieves," replied Sanit; "we rounded up all the bad characters in this district about two years ago. There was one tough fellow, named Ai Nark, who would have been after you for certain if he were still alive. He hardly ever stole anything but guns, and I see you have at least two of them with you. Any sort of firearm was irresistible to him. But he is dead and buried. I shot him myself."

As a matter of fact, I had three weapons with me; a ·303 rifle, a 12-bore shot-gun, and a small revolver. When the time came to turn in for the night, I leant my rifle

7

in one corner of the tent, laid the shot-gun, in its case, under my camp cot, and put the revolver under my pillow.

I had not been asleep for very long before I was aroused by the sound of something falling. Turning on my flashlight, I saw that my rifle had fallen over from its place in the corner of the tent, and was being slowly drawn along the floor, stock first, underneath the canvas flap of the tent. I leapt from my cot and seized the barrel. There seemed to be a slight resistance for a moment on the part of someone outside, but this ceased almost at once, and I recovered my rifle. While this was happening, I shouted loudly for aid. All my servants, as well as several policemen, came running up. I told them what had happened, and we all went outside to search for any trace of an intruder. All we found was a stray cow, and the general consensus of opinion was that the cow had lurched against the tent, causing the rifle to fall down, and that I, in my half-awakened state, had imagined the rest.

I, however, had some faith in my own sense of sight and touch. Before retiring to sleep, I put my rifle under my mattress, so that any attempt to remove it would wake me at once. Moreover, I got my cook, who had formerly been for some years a professional boxer, to bring along his mat and sleep on the floor of the tent at my side.

I must have been sleeping for over an hour, when I was disturbed by a slight shaking of my cot, and at the same time an indistinct clicking sound from beneath me. I sprang out of bed — incidentally putting my foot on the cook's face. He jumped up pretty speedily, and together we looked under the cot. My gun-case, which had been shut with the usual sort of catch, but not locked, had been unlatched; the lid was open, and the barrel of the gun had been moved, and was lying across the section of the case containing the stock.

Once again, the Police deserted their slumbers on hearing all the talking. This time, they seemed to be more impressed than they had been in regard to the rifle, and offered to put a man on guard outside the tent; so, with my boxer-cook asleep by my side, and a policeman standing a few yards away, I once more composed myself to sleep.

8

This time, I must have slumbered for some hours. It was getting on towards daylight when I experienced a sensation as of something moving under my pillow. I gently put my hand under the pillow, and touched — not my revolver — but a hand! And such a hand! It was cold, clammy, and disgusting beyond description. All the coldness and clamminess of all the cold, clammy, unpleasant hands in the world, living or dead, seemed to be concentrated in that hateful hand.

I made no attempt to hold onto the clammy hand, but jumped once more out of bed, and yelled at the top of my voice.

*　　　*　　　*

Once again, all the camp and all the Police were aroused, but there was even less to be seen than on the former occasion. My revolver had been moved from under the pillow to the edge of the cot. That was all!

That was all. But it was enough for me. The time was now 4 a.m. I swallowed a stiff whisky and water, got out a book, and settled down to spend the rest of the night in my camp chair.

In the morning, Lieutenant Sanit, who had spent the night at his house some way off, and had heard nothing of what had happened, kindly came along to ask me what sort of a night I had had.

"Not too good," said I, "I rather fancy there was a thief hanging around with an eye on may firearms."

"Impossible!" he exclaimed, "Nothing of that kind has been heard of since the days of Ai Nark. But he is dead. I shot him and buried him myself."

"And where did you bury him, may I ask?"

"Why, right here, on this very spot."

"Do you mean to tell me that you let me put up my tent right on top of the grave of a dead robber?"

"Well, Nai, you had had all the trouble of putting it up before I came along to see you. And, anyhow, I felt quite sure there would not be any unpleasant smell, or anything like that. You see, Ai Nark has been in his grave for two years, and must be quite dry by now. Thoroughly desiccated, without the slightest doubt."

"What!" I cried. "You have the nerve to stand there and tell me that Ai Nark is dry! You have the audacity to assert that he is desiccated! Let me tell you that you do not know what you are talking about. He hasn't dried up at all! He is clammy — horribly clammy!"

RHINOCEROS BLOOD

This is a story which was told me long ago, a story of the days when the Lao Chiefs of Northern Siam still ruled their little realms with despotic power; the days when a man possessed of a stout heart and endless patience could still track down and kill a rhinoceros in the swamps near Chiengrai.

Noi Thep of Wieng Wai once actually killed a rhinoceros. True, it was a very small one, and had no horn, but still it was a real rhinoceros, and on the strength of this exploit Noi Thep enjoyed a reputation as a mighty hunter throughout his native State of Wieng Wai and in all the neighbouring Principalities.

One day Chao Lerm, the ruling Chief of Wieng Wai, an aged and rather decrepit man, sent for Noi Thep to come and see him. The interview took place in the Chief's private den. And this is what the Chief said:—

"Noi Thep, I look upon you as a faithful and loyal subject, and I want you to help me in a very important matter. As you know, I have had many wives in my time, but now they are all dead except one, and she is old. Both my sons are dead, and I have only daughters left. When I die, my brother and my eldest son-in-law will both claim the right to succeed me, and there may be civil war in the State. I have decided to marry a young wife and see if I can still beget a son to succeed me when I die. But I am old, maybe too old to have a son unless you help me. I am told by my doctors that what I need to strengthen and invigorate me is

10

the blood of a rhinoceros. Now you are a very great hunter, and have actually killed a rhinoceros. Go, I beseech you, without delay to Chiengrai and seek in the swamps near that city for a rhinoceros. Kill it, and bring back to me six bottles of its blood. If you can do this, I will confer upon you the title of "Muen" and pay you a hundred Rupees. If I later become the father of a son, I will pay you a further sum of five hundred Rupees and bestow upon you the title of "Saen."

Noi Thep bent his head to the earth, and replied:—

"Father Chief, your word is law. Tomorrow I leave for Chiengrai. Within one month at most you shall have six bottles of rhinoceros blood."

So Noi Thep set forth on his quest, far from easy in his mind. It was by no means certain that he would be able to track down and kill a rhinoceros, which even in those days was a rare sort of animal. He well knew that, if he failed, instead of receiving a bag of Rupees and a title of nobility, he was likely to be soundly thrashed or put in the lock-up — or both.

When Noi Thep reached Chiengrai, he went to consult his cousin, Poo Khat, who was also a celebrated hunter. Poo Khat looked grave.

"My dear cousin," said he, "your position is serious. It is most improbable that you will succeed in bagging a rhino-ceros. Two of them were shot last month. I do not think there are any more to be found near here now. But I have a plan, which may perhaps solve your problem. I am about to slaughter a buffalo. Why not take back some buffalo blood to your Father Chief? He will never be able to tell the difference. Moreover, by a lucky chance, this particular buffalo has one very peculiar horn, all stunted and gnarled. If we hack it about a bit, you ought to be able to pass it off as a rhinoceros horn. So cheer up! Your fortune is as good as made."

Noi Thep greeted this suggestion with warm enthusiasm. The buffalo was duly slaughtered, a dozen (not six) bottles were filled with its blood, and its stunted horn was skilfully fixed up to look as much as possible like the nasal appendage of a rhinoceros. Then Noi Thep settled down to enjoy a couple of weeks at Chiengrai, beating it up with his cousin, and sampling all the gaieties of that comparatively great metropolis.

He returned to Wieng Wai exactly one month after he had started on his journey. He at once went to see the old Chief. Kneeling before him, he placed at his feet the twelve bottles of buffalo blood and the stunted horn. Then, with tears in his eyes, he related his adventures:—

"I spent," said Noi Thep, "seventeen days in the Chiengrai swamps eating nothing but glutinous rice and wild berries, and devoured day and night by leeches and mosquitos. I was attacked thrice by cobras and chased four times by tigers. But what did I care? I reminded myself that I was there to carry out a duty entrusted to me by my beloved Father Chief, and I laughed at every danger and hardship. And here I am, safe and sound, with twelve bottles of invigorating rhinoceros blood, instead of only six, and also a beautiful rhinoceros horn."

In a voice filled with emotion, the old Chief replied:— "Noi Thep, you are a brave man and a faithful servant. Here is a bag containing two hundred Rupees, double the amount I promised you, and I confer upon you the noble title of Muen. And now I will prepare for my marriage. I have decided to take unto myself Nang Bua Thep, a very beautiful and virtuous girl, and a relative of your aunt by marriage."

"Muen" Thep showed no outward sign of disturbance on hearing this news, but inwardly he was filled with rage and disappointment. Nang Bua Thip was a young lady whom he had often met at the house of his aunt, and whom he greatly admired. It had occurred to him more than once that when he had a title of nobility and a bag of Rupees, she might probably look upon him as a suitable husband.

Bidding a humble and grateful farewell to the old Chief, Muen Thep repaired to the house of his aunt, and to her he unburdened his soul.

"Just think," said he in disgust, "I have endured frightful hardships and run unspeakable risks in order to procure rhinoceros blood for the Father Chief, and now he intends to take unto himself the very girl I have had my eye on for months past."

12

"Never mind," replied his aunt; "although Nang Bua Thip cannot be your wife, you will still be able to see her from time to time. She has promised me that when she is married she will often come to see me, as she has always been in the habit of doing. I will let you know when she is here. Then you will be able to drop in and have a chat with her, as you used to do. You may as well come in through the back garden, so as to avoid attracting needless attention."

So the old Chief fed himself up on rhinoceros blood and married a pretty young wife. And his pretty wife often went to visit her old friend. And her old friend's nephew often dropped in for a chat — coming through the back garden.

In less than a year, Nang Bua Thip presented her aged husband with a fine, healthy son and heir.

The old Chief was overjoyed. Public celebrations were held throughout the State of Wieng Wai, gifts presented to every priest in the capital, and hundreds of great rockets let off.

At the height of the festivities, the Chief sent for Muen Thep and said to him:—

"Muen Thep, you have done more for me than any other man in my realm. It is through you, and you alone, that I now have a son and heir to succeed me. I only regret that you had to suffer so much hardship and pain in my service. I now confer upon you the noble title of Saen, and I present you with a bag containing one thousand Rupees instead of the five hundred I promised you."

"Saen" Thep knelt once more at the old Chief's feet, and weepingly replied:—

"I cannot thank you enough, Father Chief, for the honourable title you have conferred upon me, and the munificent gift of money. But do not, I beg, speak of danger and suffering. Anything I have done to assist you in realising your hope of having a son and heir to succeed you has been a real pleasure and delight to me; and you may rely upon me to continue to serve you to the best of my ability as long as you may live."

And so he did. And when, only a year later, the old Chief dead, he remembered Saen Thep in his will, bequeathing

13

to him a house and land, a sum of ten thousand Rupees —
and the rhinoceros horn. And Saen Thep married Nang Bua
Thep and lived happily ever after.

FEEDING THE FISHES

There is a little pool just outside the entrance to the
great cave at Chiengdao in Northern Siam. A limpid stream
flows into it from the cave, coming from some hidden spring
far in the heart of the Chiengdao mountain, and lapping the
feet of the great Buddha in the cave. For hundreds of years
there have been fishes swimming in the pool, fat carp with
pink bellies and silver fins, one generation after another, fear-
less of hook or net, safe and free under the protection of the
Lord Buddha.

I camped close to the mouth of the cave one cold night
long ago. Before turning in, I took my usual stroll round
the camp, and said a few words to the clerks, syces and
elephant men. I observed that Nai Sang, my assistant clerk,
was cooking a fish in a large frying pan. Nai Sang was a
young man who liked to pose as a free-thinker, and was wont
to talk in contemptuous terms about what he called foolish
superstitions. For a moment the thought struck me that he
had caught one of the sacred fishes, but I almost instantly
dismissed the idea as absurd, since it was a thing which nobody would think of doing. Nevertheless, I asked Nai Sang
where he had bought the fish. "In the market of Chiengdao
village, as we passed through," he replied. Maybe I still felt
a trifle uneasy, but I said no more, left Nai Sang to his
cookery and turned in.

After I had been back in Chiengmai for a few weeks, I
noticed a change in Nai Sang. He had become thin, and
seemed tired and listless. Moreover, he was working very
badly, made constant mistakes, and appeared to be going
about in a sort of dream. I sent him to the Mission doctor,
who dosed him with a tonic, but it did him no good. He

grew thinner and paler, and muddled his work more and more. At last I called him into my private office and suggested that he should take a month's leave of absence and go up to stay at the little Consular bungalow on Doi Suthep mountain.

Nai Sang broke down completely and knelt at my feet weeping. Then he said:

"Nai, it is useless for me to take a holiday. I am dying, and no treatment or medicine can save me. There is a curse on me which nothing can remove. Do you remember, when we camped at Chiengdao, you asked me about the fish you saw me frying, and I told you I had bought it in the market? That was a lie! It was one of the sacred fishes from the pool outside the Buddha's cave. I knew that nobody ever dared to molest those fishes, but I told myself that I should be a fool to let an idle superstition deprive me of a good supper. So I crept along to the pool after dusk, baited a hook with a lump of pork, and almost instantly caught a large fish. Now I realise it was a terrible sin, for which I must pay with my life. I am slowly dying, and when I am dead my soul will be tormented in hell for thousands of years."

"Listen, Nai Sang," said I. "What you did was certainly very wrong. I myself, though I am not a Buddhist, would think it wrong to catch and eat a fish from a pool which has been regarded as sacred for nearly a thousand years. But we Christians believe that our sins will be forgiven if we truly repent, and try to do what we can to make restitution. You are a Buddhist, but I am sure that for you, too, pardon is possible if you know how to seek it. Why not consult the head priest at Wat Chalerm? He is a very venerable and holy man, and I am sure he will give you good advice."

A few days later, Nai Sang came to me again, and asked me for one month's leave of absence, which I readily granted him.

At the end of the month, Nai Sang reappeared. He came into my office looking quite like his old self, plump and cheerful. When I was about to shake hands with him, he put out his left hand, and I then noticed that his right hand was wrapped up in a bandage. And this is the tale he told me:

15

"....laid the forefinger of my right hand on the railing and with one sharp stroke of the axe cut it off..."

"I took your advice, Nai, and went to consult the head priest at Wat Chalerm. He told me that my sin was very great, but that I could obtain peace and forgiveness if I gave the sacred fishes something belonging to myself which I valued and could ill spare.

"The next day I set forth for Chiengdao, intending to cast my gold ring, the most valuable thing I possess, into the pool of the sacred fishes. I arrived there at dusk on the third day out, and went into the cave to pray to the image of the Lord Buddha. When I had confessed my sin, I took off my ring and laid it before the image, saying that I was about to throw it into the pool as a token of repentance. Then, when I looked at the little ring, lying there in front of the great image, the thought struck me that it was really a paltry and worthless thing, which meant little to me. Had I lost it, I would hardly have shed a tear.

"So I picked it up, and as I did so, I bethought myself that though the ring was but a useless ornament, my fingers were not. If I sacrificed one of my fingers, I should be giving something which I should miss every day until the end of my life. So I went out again and stood on the bridge which spans the sacred pool. Then I saw a man nearby, cutting firewood with a small axe. I went to him and asked for his axe. I returned to the bridge, holding the axe in my left hand, laid the forefinger of my right hand on the railing, and with one sharp stroke of the axe cut it off, and let it fall into the pool. I felt sick and faint when my finger came off, but the woodcutter was very good to me. He tore up his shirt to bandage my hand, and helped me to walk back to the village. There I met a doctor, who let me stay in his house, and treated my hand carefully for a week, and my wound healed quickly.

"From the moment when my finger fell into the pool, my mind was at peace. I forgot the pain and weakness, for I knew in my heart that I would not die, but would soon be well and strong again. And here I am, stronger and more active than ever before, and my hand almost healed. I am ready to start work again tomorrow."

So Nai Sang returned to work. He soon became a first class clerk, and was known throughout Northern Siam as a

17

soccer player and a good amateur boxer. He is still alive today, hale and hearty, with a large family of children and grand-children. But he has one peculiarity. He never goes fishing, and he never eats fish.

THE WERE-MOUSE

Lung Wan and his son Noi Liem lived together in a little house close to the compound of the Metropolitan Bank of Thailand at Chiengmai. Lung Wan's wife had died some years before the date of this story, so the two of them looked after themselves and one another. Lung Wan was night watch-man at the Bank, and Noi Liem was the manager's cook. In their spare time they cultivated fruit and vegetables in their small garden. Lung Wan was sixty years of age, and his son twenty-one.

One afternoon, when Lung Wan got up from his bed — for he slept in the daytime — his son came to him in a state of great excitement. "Father," he said, "when I was digging a hole in our garden just now, to plant our new lamyai tree, I found a box buried deep in the earth. I opened it, and inside it I found this piece of lead piping. What do you think it is?"

The old man examined the pipe. It was a section of ordinary lead piping about a foot long, the two ends of which had been hammered down so as to render them watertight.

"We will soon find out," said Lung Wan. "Bring me an axe."

When Noi Liem brought an axe, it was a simple matter to hack off one end of the pipe and to extract its contents. These proved to be two strips of palm-leaf, of the type used in former days when paper was scarce. On them, scratched with a stylus, were twenty or thirty lines of writing in the old Lao characters.

"My son," said Lung Wan, "when you were a novice in

18

the temple, you learnt to read this sort of writing; see whether you can make anything of it."

So that night, after he had finished his work, Noi Liem sat down and set himself to transcribe the inscription into modern Thai.

This is what he read: "Seventh day of the waxing moon, fourth month of the year of the goat 1200 (A.D. 1838). I, Chao Nan Inta, who was known in my youth to be a were-tiger, being about to die, have written down the method to be followed by those who desire to change their forms into those of animals. But be it known to him who finds this scroll that the charm may bring about different changes in different men. A man, like myself, of fierce character, may become a tiger, a man of pre-eminent merit and wisdom may be transformed into an elephant, a man of low and worthless character may turn into a scorpion or centipede. So let the finder of this beware of the danger he runs in the event of his changing himself into some creature which is easily destroyed. Moreover, let him remember that he can retain his changed form for only six hours at a time."

Then followed the formula. A potion brewed from seven different herbs had first to be swallowed, then the body rubbed all over with an unguent made of seven varieties of fat — most of them of a terrible and revolting kind. After that, one had to stand in a circle drawn to a specified design, and pronounce seven magic words.

Imagine the excitement of Lung Wan and Noi Liem. The old fellow exclaimed: "This must have been written by my great-grandfather. I have heard it said that he bore the reputation of being a were-tiger! You must test this formula as soon as possible, my son. I am too old to play about with mysteries such as these."

Noi Liem was quite ready to risk the experiment. "I think it very probable," he said, "that I shall turn into an elephant. You can then take me and sell me for a very high price to one of the timber firms. Six hours later I shall revert to my original form and come back home. If we do this trick three or four times, our fortune is made."

During the following few weeks, father and son spent all their spare time seeking out the ingredients needed for the magic spell. At last, when all was in order, they prepared to carry out the transformation.

The two rash experimenters repaired to the vegetable garden behind their house. Noi Liem swallowed the evil-tasting mixture, smeared himself all over with the noxious ointment, stood inside the magic circle, took a deep breath, and uttered the seven fateful words. His father stood anxiously by, uncertain whether he would see the young man expand into an elephant, or begin to exhibit the yellow and black stripes of a tiger.

Nothing of the sort happened. On the contrary, Noi Liem began to shrink. He shrank and shrank, grew smaller and smaller, sprouted whiskers and a long tail, and in about three minutes there was no possibility of mistaking what had happened. The young fellow had turned into a mouse!

Lung Wan was bitterly disappointed. What, thought he, is the use of a mouse, even a were-mouse? There is no money to be made out of a mouse. Moreover, a dog or a cat may destroy it in a moment. This thought terrified him. He seized the mouse, ran quickly back into the house, and put the little creature into a strong teak box. After boring a few air-holes in the lid, and putting in a little rice for his son to eat, he went over to the Bank to start his night's vigil there.

When he returned home next morning, Lung Wan found that the box had been burst open, and his son was just start-ing out to purchase his master's supply of food for the day. I need hardly say that Lung Wan did not get much sleep that morning, while Noi Liem concocted such atrocious food for Mr. Tenby, the Bank Manager, and his wife, that he was threatened with dismissal.

Later in the day, when he had had time to think things over, Lung Wan said to his son: "My dear boy, it certainly was a great shock to me when I saw you turning into a mouse. But I have now had time to think things over, and I have worked out a plan, which, if we are careful, ought to be even more profitable than our scheme for selling you, in the form of an elephant, to a timber firm. In the Bank's strong-room there are many bundles of currency notes. Some bundles — those on the top shelf — contain notes of the value of 1,000 bahts each. Behind the strong-room, where I am stationed on guard, there is a very small ventilation grid, consisting of four iron bars. These bars are far enough apart to permit of a small mouse creeping in between them. You shall become a mouse again next Saturday. The spell lasts for six hours. Allowing a margin of two hours for safety, we shall have four hours in which to work. I will put you through the grid, and you will then push out to me as many thousand baht notes as you can get hold of in four hours. I should say you ought to be able to manage one every two minutes. The elephant trick is nothing to this."

"I have suggested Saturday, bacause the manager and Mrs. Tenby, who live over the Bank, are dining out that night, so he cannot come snooping round late at night, as he often does, to see that everything is all right. He will not be back before midnight, so if we start operations at eight o'clock, we shall have plenty of time. Moreover, Monday and Tuesday are public holidays, so the bank will be closed, and there is no chance of the loss being discovered before Wednesday. Thus we shall have three clear days in which to put the money in a place of safety. But anyhow, there will be no finger-marks or other traces to connect us with the missing notes. In fact, the whole thing will look like an inside job."

Noi Liem readily agreed. The magic draught and oint-ment were prepared, and on the Saturday night Noi Liem stood once more in the magic circle and uttered the seven cryptic words. The transformation was successfully accom-plished, and Lung Wan went across to take up his station at the back of the bank strong-room, carrying his son in his pocket.

A few minutes after eight o'clock, Mr. and Mrs. Tenby came down from their flat, got into their car, and were driven away. As soon as the car was out of sight, Lung Wan stood on the three-legged stool provided by the Bank for his use, took the little mouse from his pocket, and let it slip in between the bars of the ventilator grid of the strong-room. Then he stood and waited for a thousand baht note to fall out through the grid. No note came through, but after a few moments a sound was heard which made the watcher's heart stand still and his blood run cold — the *miaow* of a cat.

21

Then the miserable man remembered, all too late, that a few months previously the manager's cat had inadvertently been locked in the strong-room, and the manager had come down at midnight to release it. The same thing had clearly happened again — and on this of all nights. In an agony of fear, he stood on the stool and whispered through the grid: "Come back, my son, come back at once."

Too late! In a moment he heard a loud *miaow*, then a feeble squeak. An instant later, the squeak was merged into a groaning sound, clearly coming from a human throat. Then the cat began to scream — the frantic, agonised scream of a terrified animal.

The manager's houseboy, who was sleeping upstairs, came rushing down. The laundress and her husband, who lived in a small house near by, came running out. Soon there was a small crowd, all listening in consternation to the frightful screams of the maddened cat in the strong-room. Now and then there was a lull, but after a few moments the terrified cat started to scream again. This went on until after midnight. Lung Wan was trembling all over and streaming with sweat. Well he knew what must have happened in the strong-room, but he could not share his knowledge with the bystanders. All he could say was: "Something seems to have frightened the cat."

A little after midnight, Mr. and Mrs. Tenby came home. Lung Wan, surrounded by a crowd of excited people, awaited them. Pale and trembling, he staggered up to the manager, and said: "Please go at once, Sir, and open the door of the strong-room. Your cat is locked up there, and is screaming so loud that it has roused the whole neighbourhood."

The manager went to his office, got out his keys, and proceeded to unlock the strong-room door. Immediately the cat, with staring eyes, and every hair standing on end, tore past him and vanished into the darkness. Then, when the door was fully opened, an astonishing sight met the eyes of Mr. Tenby, and of the throng of frightened folk who crowded in behind him. The naked body of a young man lay on the cement floor of the room. He was dead, that was clear, and had suffered the most appalling injuries. His skull was crushed

22

in, his body was bleeding from a dozen or more deep gashes, and his left arm was almost severed from his body.

"Great God!" exclaimed the manager, "it is my cook. Your son, Lung Wan."

But Lung Wan had fainted away.

"How did he get in here?" cried Mr. Tenby. "I shut the door myself, and there is nowhere where he could possibly have hidden. How did the murderer get out? There was only the cat in here. No cat, not even a full-sized tiger, could have inflicted such frightful injuries. Why, the poor fellow's skull is crushed flat, and his brains all over the floor. His arm is snapped in two, and only hanging onto his body by a strip of skin. Nothing smaller than an elephant could have mangled him so."

These, and a hundred other questions, the manager asked. When a doctor was summoned, and when the Police appeared on the scene, they too, gazing in horror at the mutilated corpse of Noi Liem, were equally puzzled. But to all these questions nobody, either then or at any later time, could find a plausible answer. The whole matter remained an unsolved mystery.

*　　　*　　　*

"How then," my readers may ask, "did you find out about it?" I will tell you. I had once performed a service for Lung Wan, and when he was dying, a couple of years after the events related above, he sent for me and told me the whole story, asking me to keep it secret.

Thirty years have now gone by. Mr. and Mrs. Tenby and everyone else who was present on that fateful night, are long since dead, so I feel that no harm can be done by revealing the cause of Noi Liem's death.

So here is the truth at last.

THE FERRYMAN

Pu Inta was a ferryman. His father, his grandfather, and all his forbears had been ferrymen. From one generation to

23

another he had worked the ferry known as "Mango Tree Ferry," carrying passengers to and fro across the Me Ping River at Chiengmai, three miles below the bridge. Everyone knows the ferry, and everyone knows Pu Inta.

Day by day, from dawn till dusk, and often later, if needed, Pu Inta was at work, poling his boat in the dry weather, rowing it during the rains, ever and ever from bank to bank. Pu Inta was proud of his ferry and loved his work. He felt that he was doing a useful job, and doing it well. But he had one sorrow. He was growing old, and his only son was a cripple.

The lad, Noi Boon, was fifteen years of age — a good boy, clever at his books and a skilled musician. He could play the xylophone, the flute and the banjo, and had a fine singing voice. But he was a cripple — his back was bent and he had one leg shorter than the other. He could never be a ferry-man.

Pu Inta never let his son know of the sorrow in his heart. He worked away at the ferry, ostensibly cheerful and happy, but always tormented by the thought, "One day I must die or grow too old for work, and then this ancient ferry will pass into the hands of strangers.

*   *   *

One day, there was a fair at the village temple. The ferryman's wife, Nang Keow, and her daughter, Bua Kham, decided to run a refreshment stall at the fair, selling curry and rice, tea and coffee, cakes and soft drinks. The stall was a great success. All the village people knew the ferryman's wife and daughter, and all of them flocked to the stall.

After a time, Nang Keow noticed a tall, good-looking young soldier, who kept passing to and fro in front of her stall, but seemed hesitant about stopping to buy anything. When he was passing for the fifth or sixth time, she called out, "Nai, come and try some of my curry. I can guarantee it." The soldier stopped and came to the stall. After sampling the curry — which he pronounced excellent — he ate a few cakes, and then started to drink cup after cup of coffee. In fact, having once made up his mind to visit the stall, he seemed quite unable to tear himself away, and Nang Keow could not

24

help noticing that his eyes were all the time fixed on her daughter.

"Tell me, Madam," asked the soldier, after his seventh cup of coffee, "do you live here near the temple?"

"Not very near," answered Nang Keow. "My house is on the banks of the river. I am the wife of the ferryman."

When he heard these words, the young soldier's face lit up. "Ferryman!" he exclaimed, "that is a fine job. I think a lot of ferrymen. Do you suppose your husband would let me come to call on him and have a look at his ferry? My name is Tawee, and I assure you that I am a respectable young man."

By this time, Nang Keow had sized up the young fellow pretty well. He clearly had plenty of money to spend — he had a racing bicycle leaning against a tree near by, and was wearing an expensive-looking wrist-watch. Moreover, he wore his uniform with the slight swagger of a man accustomed to being smartly dressed. Apart from this, she had not failed to observe that her daughter was by no means unaware of the interest she had aroused in the young man, and showed no signs of resenting it.

So she said, "Come along any time you like, Nai Tawee; I am sure my husband will be glad to see you."

A few evenings later, when Tawee was able to get leave from the barracks, he put in an appearance at the ferryman's house, bringing two big bunches of orchids for Nang Keow and her daughter, and a bottle of Mekong whisky for her husband.

Pu Inta took an instant liking to Nai Tawee. After a little polite conversation, the visitor was taken to see the ferry-boat. He praised the boat, the new bamboo landing-stage, the ferryman's house, and everything about the place. "Yours is the finest and most useful job in the world, Uncle," said he.

"It is good of you to say that, young Nai," said Pu Inta. "I will admit that I love my ferry and am proud of it. It has been the property of my family for many generations. But, alas! my son is not strong and can never be a ferryman, so when I die or have to stop work, the ferry will pass into the hands of strangers."

25

"But you have a daughter, Uncle. She is beautiful girl, and is sure to get married before long. Why should her husband not take over the ferry from you when you pass away or become too old to work?"

"I fear that is unlikely," replied the old man. "There are but few ferryman in the world, and I can hardly hope that my daughter will marry one of them."

"Let us go up to your house," said Tawee. "We will broach the bottle I have brought with me, and, over a glass of Mekong, I will make a proposal which I hope will not displease you."

*　　　　*　　　　*

So they went up to the house, and Tawee, after some hesitation, said to the ferryman:

"Uncle, if your son cannot carry on the ferry after you have gone, would not a son-in-law, and a son-in-law, moreover, who is an expert ferryman, do almost as well? Look at me! I am a tall, strong fellow, and have worked at the ferry over the Me Kuang River at Lampoon, sixteen miles away from here, ever since I was ten years old. My father owns that ferry, and it has been handed down in our family for generations, just like your ferry. My blood is ferryman's blood, and my bones are ferryman's bones. But my father does not depend on me. I have an elder brother who is married and has two sturdy boys. He will take over our ferry when the time comes."

"I have a feeling that your daughter does not dislike me. If I can persuade her to marry me, I will be another son to you and will help you as long as you live, and take over from you when the time comes for you to say goodbye. Do not think, because I am smartly dressed and have an expensive bicycle and wrist-watch, that I am afraid, of doing a hard day's work. When a man is in the Army, he likes to swank about a bit. In a month, my term of service will be over. Let me marry your daughter, if she will agree, and I promise you I will be a good husband and good ferryman. Moreover, I shall not enter your family empty-handed. My father is not a poor man. He will certainly give me my share of his estate when I marry."

*　　　　*　　　　*

26

Pu Inta could hardly believe his ears. All his troubles seemed to have vanished in a moment. Here was a smart, tall, handsome young man, with plenty of money, asking to marry his daughter. But better than all else, the young man was a real ferryman, the descendant of generations of ferrymen, just like himself. Nevertheless, Pu Inta remembered one thing.

"Nai Tawee," he said, "I will not deny that your proposal is very pleasing to me. But I must lay down one condition. My son, Noi Boon, must be provided for. You must promise me that he shall always have a third share of the takings of the ferry."

"Of course I will promise that," exclaimed Tawee. "Moreover, why should not Noi Boon take a share in the business? My father has a refreshment stall on the banks of the river near our ferry, run by my sister and my younger brother. Your wife and daughter are clever business women. I could see that from their stall at the fair. We will open up a stall here, and your son can help to run it. It will all be part of the ferry, so he will be a ferryman too, even though he cannot row or pole the boat. Ferryman all!"

And it all fell out according to Tawee's plan. Bua Kham needed very little persuasion to accept Tawee as her husband, and today any visitor to "Mango Tree Ferry" can see two born ferrymen, old Pu Inta and young Tawee, rowing or poling their boat turn and turn about, while crippled Noi Boon is perfectly happy, helping his mother and sister with the refreshment stall on the river bank. And the last time I crossed by the ferry, I noticed a plump young budding ferryman crawling about the place on all fours.

They are the most contented family for miles around.

STRANGE PASSENGER

Nai Wichien Prasert was a tough chap. Tough and plucky. He was well known as a boxer in Northern Thailand in the early post-war years, and when the Government decided to send an expeditionary force to help the United Nations against the Communist aggressors in Korea, he was among the first to volunteer for service. He returned from the war with two Thai and one United States medals for gallantry, but to offset these honourable awards he had acquired a glass eye and a game right leg.

However, Nai Wichien was not the sort of man to lead an idle life. He had saved a bit of money, and he sold a bit of land, and he invested all his capital in a Chevrolet motor-bus, which he ran between Chiengmai and Muang Ngai, a distance of some ninety miles, carrying freight and passengers both ways. With his glass eye and his game leg he could not obtain a driving license, but he took on his young cousin Taworn as driver, and in a short time was doing extremely well. Everybody wanted to patronise the bus of a man who was both a popular boxer and a war hero.

In those days Wichien was a well-known figure along the Northern road, wearing a black zip-jacket, a yellow leather cap with an extra long peak, and dark goggles.

One cold night in January, Wichien's bus was making the return trip from Muang Ngai to Chiengmai. As a rule, drivers prefer not to make this journey by night, but there had been some engine trouble, which had caused a delay of three hours, and it was eleven o'clock when they reached a spot about half way to Chiengmai, where there are some hot sulphur springs.

Suddenly, Taworn saw the trunk of a small tree lying across the road a short way ahead. He slowed down, then stopped. Immediately two men, both holding automatic pistols, came out from the jungle at the side of the road. One of them called out: "Driver to hold up his hands and step down." Wichien was sitting beside the driver. He quickly got out a revolver which he kept under the seat, and jumped down from the bus. As soon as his feet touched the ground, he pointed his revolver at the head of the foremost of the two robbers. "Curse you, you filthy dog," he cried, "would you dare to hold up my bus?" Saying this, he fired. The robber returned his fire almost in the same instant. But Wichien, though a brave man, was an indifferent shot. More-over, his glass eye and his dark goggles were not conducive to accurate aim. The robber was unhurt, but Wichien fell down mortally wounded. The robber stepped forward and kicked the dying man, calling out as he did so: "Does anyone else want a bullet? I have plenty left."

Young Taworn jumped down from his seat, holding up his hands Then all the passengers were made to alight and stand in a row, guarded by the second robber, while the first ruffian ransacked the bus. In the end, they got only a few hundred bahts, some trinkets from the female passengers, and half a dozen watches. Disappointed, the first robber gave Wichien another kick. The dying man sat up, and said: "I know you; you are Tiger Rawt, wanted by the Police of five Provinces. I'm dying, but I will get even with you yet. Daring to stop my bus!" The robber put a bullet through his brain.

Then the two ruffians went off into the forest with their loot. The driver and passengers dragged away the tree trunk, and the bus, bearing its dead owner, went on its way.

The man known as Tiger Rawt was suspected of having been concerned in a number of robberies and murders all over Thailand In the course of these, a Chinese merchant had been murdered near Chumporn in the Peninsula, and a Thai Police Major wounded in the Chiengrai district. But the death of Nai Wichien, who was a well-known and popular man in Northern Thailand, caused a good deal of excitement. The Government offered a reward of five thousand bahts for the murderer's body, dead or alive, and this sum was doubled by the proprietor of a local newspaper. During the following year three cases occurred in which motor-buses were held up and looted in various parts of the Kingdom, but though it was suspected that Tiger Rawt was responsible for all these crimes, he continued to evade capture.

Wichien's bus was sold to a local syndicate, who continued to run it between Chiengmai and Muang Ngai, and retained young Taworn as driver.

*   *   *

About two years after the murder of Wichien, it so happened that the bus was once more delayed at Muang Ngai, and was returning to Chiengmai after dark. As they

29

were passing through a small village a few miles from the Hot Springs, a man signalled to them to stop. He was wearing a black zip-jacket, with the collar turned up round his neck, a yellow leather cap with an unusually long peak, and dark goggles. When the bus stopped, he jumped up onto the front seat and took his place beside the driver.

"How far are you going?" asked Taworn. "Only as far as the Hot Springs," was the reply. Taworn was startled. He could not see the stranger's face, but his style of dress, his general appearance and particularly his voice, reminded him of his murdered cousin and employer, Nai Wichien.

"Why do you want to go to the Hot Springs?" he asked, "there is nothing there but hot water."

"I have an important appointment there," said the stranger.

"Excuse my mentioning it, Sir," said Taworn, "but you quite startled me just now. Your appearance is very much like that of my former employer, Nai Wichien Prasert, who was killed by robbers not far from here."

But the stranger only grunted.

A few minutes later Taworn, to his horror and dismay, once again saw a tree trunk lying across the road. Before slowing down, he got out his revolver, saying to the stranger as he did so: "This time I will have a shot at those devils, even if they kill me."

"Do not shoot yet," said the stranger; "leave me to manage this business. Shoot when I tell you."

Saying this, he jumped down from the bus. As before, two men came forward from the jungle. "Hands up!" cried Tiger Rawt — for he it was.

"Dog Rawt," said the stranger, "would you dare to stop my bus? Shoot away!"

The robber fired. The bullet passed through the stranger's breast, and lodged in the side of the bus.

"Shoot again! Keep on shooting all night!"

Saying this, the stranger turned down the collar of his jacket, pushed back his cap and advanced towards the robber. The latter uttered a yell, flung down his pistol, and turned to flee, followed by his companion.

"Shoot now, shoot quickly," cried the stranger. "I will guide your hand."

Taworn shot twice. Both the fleeing robbers fell.

"Well aimed, little brother!" said the stranger.

*   *   *

They took up the dead bodies of Tiger Rawt and his companion onto the bus, dragged aside the tree trunk, and made ready to continue their journey. But the stranger was nowhere to be seen. They waited some time, but he did not return, and nobody ever saw him again.

Taworn wept. "He called me 'little brother,'" said he. "He always used to call me that when he was pleased with me."

AI NOI AND THE KING

"But I do not want to sell my land, Nai, and I do not want to move my shop. This little piece of land has belonged to my ancestors for more than a hundred years, and I will not sell it. Moreover, my little cake-shop is opposite to the Police station, and all the policemen come in to buy my cakes. If I move away, I shall lose half my customers."

Thus spoke Nang Puan, of Wieng Papao, a tiny city fifty miles north of Chiengmai. She was addressing Khun Wiset, the Nai Amphur. And he answered her in angry tones.

"You are a foolish and obstinate woman, Nang Puan. I have received orders from the High Commissioner to build a new office, and I cannot find any other site so suitable as this. All the other landowners involved have agreed to sell; only you and Chek Seng have raised difficulties. He is a Chinese, so cannot be expected to show any public spirit. But you are Thai, and it is your duty to help the Government, instead of worrying me with all sorts of senseless arguments."

31

Here Chek Seng, who was standing by, interposed:— "I may be only a poor Chinese but I too have a right to justice. The sum you have offered me for my land is less than half what I paid for it. Why am I to be treated so unfairly? I will appeal to the King!"

The Nai Amphur laughed heartily at this remark. "You are an idiotic fool," said he; "appeal to the King, indeed! The King is a very great man, and lives far away. He has no time to waste over the affairs of ignorant village people like you and Nang Puan. Shut your mouth, take the money I am offering you, and stop pestering me."

So saying, the Nai Amphur strode angrily away. But the words spoken by the Chinese stuck in the mind of little Ai Noi, the nine-year-old son of Nang Puan. "Mother," he asked when they got home, "is it true what Chek Seng said? Is it possible for poor people like us to appeal to the King to help us if we are unjustly treated?"

"My son," replied Nang Puan, "I fear what Khun Wiset said is true. The King is a very good and just man, but he is too important to be troubled with the affairs of humble people like us."

So Nang Puan and Chek Seng were turned out of their land, paid a small sum in compensation, and the Nai Amphur forgot all about the matter. So did Chek Seng, who had never really contemplated the possibility of appealing to the King.

But Ai Noi did not forget. His mother opened a new shop, some way off. Her customers dwindled in numbers, and she often had difficulty in supporting herself and her little son. And every night little Ai Noi lay awake, wondering whether, after all, it might not be possible to ask for help from the great, powerful King who lived so far, far away. And every day he looked at the picture of the King which hung on the wall of his mother's shop, and thought to himself:— "He has a kind face. I am sure he would help us if he knew about our troubles."

Two months passed by. Then, one morning, Ai Noi made up his mind. He would go to Bangkok and see the King. He told nobody of this resolve, but began secretly to save money to finance his trip. At last, when he had collected a sum of three *theps*, (as rupees are called in Northern Siam) and twenty-four atts, he set forth on his adventurous journey. At that time, bahts were hardly known in the North, and stangs had not yet been invented. Apart from his small capital, Ai Noi possessed an unusual accomplishment, by means of which he hoped to be able to earn a few atts on his way. He could turn somersaults!

Over the high mountains and through the deep and swift streams the little boy made his way. When he passed through a village, he would turn a few somersaults in the street. People were astonished to see this funny little boy, seeming to appear from nowhere, turning somersaults. Northern Thai villagers are very kind-hearted people, and our small hero soon increased his capital to five *theps*, and never lacked for food or lodging. "Who are you, little boy," he was constantly asked, "and where are you going?" And he always replied:— "My name is Ai Noi, and I am going to Bangkok to see the King."

At last, after five days, Ai Noi arrived at Chiengmai. In that year of 1907, the northern capital was still a very quiet, dreamy city. No cars, no motor-buses, no electric light, only about two bicycles. Traffic consisted of a few pony-carts and ox-wagons. But to the little lad from Wieng Papao it seemed a marvellous metropolis. After crossing the somewhat shaky wooden bridge which at that time spanned the river Me Ping, he came to a two-storied brick building. In front of it was standing a tall, elderly man, of imposing appearance. "This man has a big house; he must be rich," thought Ai Noi, "I may get as much as a salung out of him for a few somersaults." So he started his gymnastic display. The elderly gentleman laughed heartily, and gave him the enormous sum of two salungs. Then he asked the usual question, "Who are you, little boy, and where are you going?" And Ai Noi replied:— "My name is Ai Noi, and I am going to Bangkok to see the King."

At that moment a small dog-cart drew up close by, and a tall, stalwart young man got out. Ai Noi had never seen a European, but he had seen pictures of them, and he at once realised that this was a *farang*. He stared open-mouthed at the new-comer. The *farang* shook hands with the tall gentle-

33

man, and said:— "Good day, Khun Luang Anusarn. I have come to ask you when your boat will be leaving for Paknampoh. I am going down river myself in a few days, and thought it might be convenient if our boats were to go down together, as there have been several cases of armed robbery near Raheng."

"That can easily be arranged, Mr. Macfie," answered Luang Anusarn. "My boat is leaving in two days. I hope that is not too early for you?"

The man addressed as Mr. Macfie was about to reply, when Ai Noi decided that the moment had arrived for him to turn a few somersaults. His performance delighted Mr. Macfie and Luang Anusarn. "Who are you, little boy," asked the former, "and where are you going?" and he received the usual reply:— "My name is Ai Noi, and I am going to Bangkok to see the King."

Mr. Macfie laughed again, and asked:—"How do you intend to get to Bangkok?"

"I will walk there," said Ai Noi. "I have walked from Wieng Papao, and I can walk to Bangkok easily enough."

"My poor little boy," said Mr. Macfie. "You cannot walk all the way to Bangkok. It would take you months. Nobody ever walks to Bangkok. They travel by boat. I am going down to Paknampoh by boat in a couple of days. Would you not like to come in my boat? I can find a corner for a little chap like you."

"That would be very kind of you, Chao," answered Ai Noi. "I would like to go in your boat, and I can pay you five *theps* for the trip."

"Never mind about the fare," said Mr. Macfie, laughing. "I will not make any charge. You can help to sweep and clean the boat, and I will feed you on the way. The river is well up, and we ought to reach Paknampoh in less than ten days. Come along with me now, and I will find somewhere for you to stay until we start on our journey."

So Mr. Macfie and Ai Noi took leave of Luang Anusarn. Ai Noi curled himself up on the floor of the dog-cart, and off they drove to the compound of the Borneo Company.

Two days later Mr. Macfie's boat started on its journey to the South. It was a big boat, with a crew of four rowers and a helmsman. Mr. Macfie occupied a large, half-open cabin astern, which he shared all day with the helmsman, and Ai Noi slept in the bows of the boat with the four rowers. Each night they tied up on a sandbank or near a village. On the fifth day, they reached the Me Ping rapids. The boatmen stripped themselves to cope with the raging waters and the boat was borne madly through a narrow channel of roaring, foaming billows. Right ahead stood a mighty cliff, and the boat seemed to be on the point of dashing itself against that terrible obstacle. Ai Noi hid his face, and trembled with fear, but the helmsman, with a single deft turn of his long oar, guided his craft safely away from the cliff, and brought it to rest in a quiet pool below the rapids. After that fearful experience, the journey was peaceful and uneventful until they reached Paknampoh, eleven days after leaving Chiengmai.

During the journey, Mr. Macfie several times asked Ai Noi about his plan of trying to see the King. "My poor boy," he warned him, "I fear you will meet with nothing but disappointment. The King is a very great man. Even the Ministers sent to Siam by foreign Kings and Emperors cannot see him without a special appointment. His own brothers are not at liberty to walk in and speak to him whenever they feel inclined to do so. How will you find anyone who is able and willing to introduce you, a little country-bred boy, into His Majesty's presence?" But Ai Noi was full of confidence. "I will manage it somehow," said he.

At Paknampoh Mr. Macfie arranged with a Chinese friend, who ran a line of steam-launches between that town and Bangkok, to take Ai Noi on one of his launches, and to feed him during the three days trip to the capital. So our young hero took leave of his kind-hearted *farang* friend, and set forth on the last stage of his long journey.

If Chiengmai had appeared to Ai Noi to be a huge and bustling city, it can easily be imagined with what feelings of amazement he found himself wandering through the streets of Bangkok. Electric tramcars whizzed past him, gharries and horse-drawn wagons flew around, it seemed to him, at breakneck speed. He even saw some daring and foolhardy young men propelling themselves through the traffic on strange vehicles with only two wheels. Most marvellous of all, he saw a four-wheeled carriage which moved along at a furious speed, without having any visible means of propulsion, emitting evil-smelling fumes as it passed along. But he was not dismayed. He walked along the footpath, and when he came to an open space, he began to turn a few of his somersaults. Atts, fuangs and salungs were showered upon him, and soon people began to ask:- "Who are you, little boy, and what are you doing here?" And Ai Noi told them:- "My name is Ai Noi, and I have come to Bangkok to see the King, Please tell me where he lives."

Everybody laughed at him, thinking he was weak in the head, but one kindly old man said:— "My poor child, the King is in his palace at Dusit Park; but you cannot go to see him; only great noblemen can go to see the King."

Still, Ai Noi was not discouraged. He had travelled over four hundred miles, by land and by water, to lay his troubles at the King's feet. Now he was within a mile of the palace, and he never doubted for a moment that he would be able to carry out his plan by hook or by crook.

And so he rambled along, asking passers-by from time to time, "Where does the King live," until at last he came to the gates of Dusit Palace. Without hesitation, he started to walk boldly in through the gates, but the two guards, astonished and scandalised, quickly chased him back, and threatened to lock him up unless he cleared out and kept away. This was an unexpected rebuff, which upset all Ai Noi's plans. He sat down on the kerb, not far from the Palace gates, to think matters over. Soon he observed, standing not far off, a pony-cart, piled high with fresh, green grass. A boy only a little older than himself was standing on guard. Ai Noi went up to the boy, and asked:— "Where are you taking that grass to?"

"Into the Palace stable," answered the boy. "It is for the King's horses. I am waiting for my master, who forgot to bring his permit to pass through the Palace gates, and has gone back to fetch it."

"Let me hide under the grass," pleaded Ai Noi. "I will give you five *theps*. Here they are. And I can also give you a lot of *salungs* and *fuangs* which people gave me this morning."

"What are these *theps* made of?" asked the lad, viewing the strange coins with a suspicious eye.

"Silver; real, true silver," asserted Ai Noi. "Bite one of them and see."

The boy bit one of the rupees. It seemed like silver, and it was nearly as big as a baht. He was tempted. "Promise to tell nobody if I let you hide under the grass," he said.

It must not be supposed that this conversation was carried on so fluently as I have written it. The two boys spoke languages which differed in many respects — but in the end, they managed to understand one another, and Ai Noi solemnly gave the required promise.

A few moments later, he was thoroughly well hidden under the load of green grass. The cart-owner returned, drove his cart to the Palace gates, showed his permit, and in they went. It was dusk by this time, and when the cart reached the royal stables, Ai Noi had little difficulty in slipping down and hiding among some trees near by. There he stayed until the next morning. He had bought a few cakes at a market stall, so was not hungry.

The next morning, our bold young hero, running along when there was nobody about, and hiding when he saw anyone approaching, made his way to a clump of bushes not far from the door of the Palace. There he waited for several hours, hoping to see the King come out. As the hours passed by, many people came out of the door, but he did not recognise any of them as the man whose picture hung in his mother's shop. At last, at about eleven o'clock, there seemed to be something of a stir in front of the Palace. A number of pages and other officials came out and stood on each side of the steps. Then two young men walked down the steps. Everybody bowed very low to them, and Ai Noi decided that they must be Princes. Finally, a middle-aged man, wearing a plain white coat and a dark blue silk panung, came through the door and walked down onto the path. Everybody bowed even lower than they had done to the two young Princes, and Ai Noi knew at once that this was the King. Indeed, even had the middle-aged man been all by himself, it would have been impossible for Ai Noi to be mistaken about him. He looked like a King.

His Majesty started to walk slowly along the path. When he came near to the place where Ai Noi was hiding, our

The cart-owner returned, drove his cart to the Palace gates, showed his permit and in they went.

young hero ran out and quickly turned four somersaults only a few yards in front of him. Some of the attendants at once seized the intruder, and seemed about to handle him roughly; but the King cried out:— "Do not hurt him. He is only a little boy. I will examine him myself. Let him go."

So Ai Noi was released, and knelt on the path in front of the King. Speaking loudly and clearly, as he always did, but with infinite kindness, His Majesty asked:— "Who are you, little boy, and what are you doing here?"

Then Ai Noi blurted out his whole tale of woe. "Chao," said he (using the title of a Lao aristocrat) "My name is Ai Noi. I come from Wieng Papao, and the Nai Amphur made my mother give him her land, and she had to sell her shop, and she is very poor, and the Police do not come to her new shop, and the Nai Amphur gave her very little money, and we are very unhappy, and it isn't right or just, and I want you to help us, and people said I would never be able to see you, and I came in Mr. Macfie's boat, and I. . . ."

"Stop, stop, little boy," exclaimed the King, laughing. King Chulalongkorn's laugh was the kindest and pleasantest laugh in the world. Little Ai Noi, hearing it, began to feel completely at his ease, and started to laugh too.

"Stop, little boy," repeated the King. "I cannot understand half of what you are telling me. You must come back with me into my house, and sit down and tell me all about your troubles bit by bit, so that I shall be able to find a way of helping you." And indeed Ai Noi's speech seemed to the King almost like a foreign language. The very title *Chao,* which the little boy used, sounded strange to his ears, and even his pronouns *I, you* and *he,* were unusual and unfamiliar words. This queer, somersaulting little boy, speaking so strangely, was something altogether new to the King, and he was enjoying himself immensely. However, he was able to understand that the boy and his mother claimed to have suffered some injustice at the hands of a Nai Amphur, and he was determined to find out what it was all about, and to help the boy if it were possible to do so.

So back the whole party went into the Palace, and into the King's private study. There Ai Noi seated himself on the floor, and little by little succeeded in making his whole story clear. When the King realised what the boy wanted, he asked him:— "Why have you come all this way by yourself. Why did not your father come to see me?"

"I have no father," replied Ai Noi. "He is dead, and my mother is only a woman, so could not make such a long journey. That is a man's job."

"You must never say that you have no father," said the King. "I am your father. I am the father of all my people, and will never allow any of them, old or young, to suffer injustice if I can prevent it. In a few minutes Phya Pichit Worakarn, my High Commissioner for the Northern Provinces, is coming here to take leave of me, before setting forth by boat for Chiengmai. He leaves tomorrow, and I will place you in his care, and ask him to investigate your case, and to see that you obtain justice."

When Phya Pichit Worakarn arrived, and was ushered into the royal presence, he was surprised to see a rather untidy-looking little boy seated on the floor close to His Majesty. After the High Commissioner had received some words of advice, and a few general instructions as to the conduct of affairs in the North, the King told Ai Noi to stand up.

"This small boy, Chao Khun," said the King, "is one of your northern flock. I give him into your care. Look after him well. He has made a complaint to me about his mother's treatment by the Nai Amphur of Wieng Papao." Then His Majesty went on to relate Ai Noi's story, as far as he had been able to understand it. "As soon as you arrive in Chiengmai, send him back to Wieng Papao, accompanied by a trustworthy official, and make it clear that if the boy's mother has suffered even the slightest hardship or injustice, it is to be set right immediately."

"Your Majesty," replied Phya Pichit. "This is an order from your own lips, delivered to me personally. I will not entrust its execution to any other man. I will go to Wieng Papao myself, and will personally investigate the whole matter, and see that justice is done. This little boy shall travel with me in my own boat. Your Majesty has entrusted him to my care, and I will look after him the same as if he were my own child. Trust me in this."

40

So little Ai Noi left the King's presence hand in hand with Phya Pichit Worakarn, the most powerful man in Northern Siam, and by the next evening he was on his way up the river in the High Commissioner's luxurious houseboat. For six weeks he lived a life of ease, eating better food than he had ever eaten in his life, and sleeping at night on a more comfortable bed than he had ever known before.

After a journey lasting six weeks, the boat arrived at Chiengmai. Within three days, Phya Pichit set forth for Wieng Papao, accompanied by Ai Noi, riding on an elephant. When Nang Puan saw her little son riding along the street mounted on an elephant, she was overcome with joy, for she had no idea where he had gone to, nor whether he was alive or dead.

In a very few days, Nang Puan was presented with a new plot of land, larger than the one she had been compelled to give up, and situated alongside the Police Station — not to mention a substantial sum of money to build a new shop. Moreover, the Chinese Chek Seng, who also laid his complaint before the High Commissioner, received a fair sum for his property. So they all lived happily ever after, as the fairy-book stories say.

Let me only add that Ai Noi is still living at Wieng Papao. He has three sons, two daughters, and a whole army of grand-children. He is never tired of showing the young folk his portrait of King Chulalongkorn, and he often says to them:- "That is the great and good King who told me I must look upon him as my father. He is smiling in the picture; but his smile in the picture is not nearly so sweet as the smile I saw on his face when I went to see him in his palace."

*   *   *

THE RING

Translation of evidence taken by the District Officer of Huey Luk, Chiengmai Province, Thailand, in connection with

the disappearance of Nai Biow Thongbai, of Malai village,
Huey Luk.

Form No. 9 B.

District Office.	Huey Luk, Chiengmai Province.
Name of District Officer.	Nai Sawang Sompetch.
Date.	June 1st. B.E. 2501 (A.D. 1958)
Subject dealt with.	Disappearance of Nai Biow Thongbai.

STATEMENT OF WITNESS

Name of witness.	Nai Sing Kham Thongbai.
Age.	24.
Occupation.	Rice Farmer.
Residence.	No. 128, Malai Village, District Huey Luk, Chiengmai Province.
Wife's name.	Nang Somboon Thongbai.

STATEMENT. For three years past I have been living with
my wife and my younger brother, Nai Biow Thongbai, at
No. 128, Malai Village. My brother was aged 20 and was
unmarried. On April 24th. last, Nai Lek Vichitr, a neighbour
of ours, asked my brother and myself to clear out an old
well on a piece of land belonging to him. This land had
been lying waste for some years, and the well was full of
leaves, sticks and other rubbish. Nai Lek said he was going
to start a vegetable garden there, and wanted to use the well
for irrigation purposes. He offered to pay us ten bahts each
for the job of clearing the well.

As my brother and I were not busy at that time, we
accepted Nai Lek's offer, and the next day, April 25th., we
started work. We took with us a bamboo ladder and a large
bucket. We lowered the ladder into the well, and Nai Biow
then climbed down and put the rubbish into the bucket, which
I pulled up and emptied. The well was in a filthy state, full
of dead leaves, twigs, rotten old coconuts, and other debris.
It took us about five hours to finish the job. When the well
was clear, my brother called out to me:— "I will just feel about

42

at the bottom of the well before I come up. I have heard of people finding gold or silver in ancient wells." A few moments later he came up the ladder, and handed me a ring which he said he had found at the bottom of the well. It was very black and dirty, but when we had wiped it a bit, we could see that it was made of gold, and set with a smooth red stone. We agreed together to say nothing to anyone about the ring, fearing that Nai Lek, the owner of the land, might claim it as his property, whereas we felt that, as we had found it, we were entitled to keep it.

The ring was a very large one. Nai Biow and I both tried it on, but we could only wear it on our thumbs, as it was too big for any of our fingers.

On our way home, Nai Biow wore the ring on his thumb. We had not gone far when we stopped, turned his face towards the side of the road, and said:—"My name is Biow, Uncle, and I am returning home after doing a job of clearing out an old well."

He seemed to be talking to nobody, but when I asked him why he was doing so, he said that he had met an old man with white hair, who had asked him his name and where he was going. This made me feel very uncomfortable, as I was certain we had met no such old man, and I feared that perhaps the foul air in the well had affected my brother's brain.

When we were nearing our home, I told Nai Biow to take off the ring and put it in his pocket, as I saw no reason why we should show it to my wife. She is a very good woman, but is rather a gossip, and we had agreed to keep the finding of the ring to ourselves for the time being.

The following morning, April 26th., we had arranged to go to the forest, about two kilometres from our house, to cut firewood. The two of us rose early and started out at about seven o'clock. My brother waited until we were well on our way, and then took the ring out of his pocket and told me to wear it. I put it on my thumb, and we continued on our way. In a short time, I was startled by the sight of a large green snake, wriggling towards me on the path just ahead. I leapt aside and raised my axe, intending to strike the snake.

"What are you up to?" cried my brother, seizing my arm.

"The snake, the snake," I answered, "let me kill it!"

"Are you mad?" asked my brother, "there is no snake there."

He wrenched the axe from me, and at the same moment the ring, which was very loose, fell off my thumb to the ground. I stooped to retrieve it, and when I stood up again, the snake had vanished. I put the ring in my pocket, and we walked on, arguing with one another as to whether I really had seen a snake or not.

When we were entering the forest where we intended to cut firewood, my brother asked me to let him wear the ring for a time. I took it from my pocket and gave it to him. He, in his turn, put it on his left thumb, and we went on into the forest. After a few minutes, the time being then about eight o'clock, we came to an open clearing, in which there were only a few large trees growing. My brother stopped, and looked ahead with an appearance of surprise.

"What a beautiful little house!" he exclaimed, "I wonder when it was built. It was not here last time we came."

"What are you talking about?" I asked. "There is no house there, nor anywhere else in this part of the forest."

"Are you blind?" replied my brother. "Of course there is a most beautiful little house there. Moreover, there is a very pretty girl sitting in the verandah, and beckoning to me to go up."

When Nai Biow said this, I was filled with fear. I thought he must be going mad. I seized him by the arm and told him he was dreaming, and implored him to go no farther, but to return back home with me at once.

He tore himself away from me and ran several steps forward. Then, to my amazement, I saw him start climbing up into the air, putting his feet alternately one higher than the other, just like a man ascending a flight of steps. But there were no steps, and no house, and he seemed to be floating in the air. His two hands were raised, as though he was making a polite salute to somebody. But there was nobody there.

When Nai Biow reached what seemed to be the top of the invisible stairs, he stood still, bowed slightly, and said:— "When did you come to live here, Madam?" I saw nobody there, and heard no words in reply to this question, but Nai Biow stood there, in the air, apparently listening intently to some invisible person speaking. I watched him in great fear and distress, thinking that he must be bewitched. As I watched, his form seemed to become less clear — a misty face and limbs, and a blur of pink and white where his shirt and shorts had been. Then a mere indistinct patch of mingled shades, and in a few moments — nothing! My brother, Nai Biow, had vanished away, leaving no trace behind, except his axe, lying on the ground.

I returned home alone, filled with fear and sorrow, and wondering whether I was insane. I at once reported the matter to village Headman.

I cannot explain this matter in any reasonable way, but I feel certain it was all due to the ring which my brother found in Nai Lek's well. I myself, when I was wearing the ring, saw a snake which had no real existence. This snake, the old man to whom my brother spoke, and the little house with the pretty girl in it, were all part of the invisible world, and when he went up into the little house, he too became one of the inhabitants of the invisible world, and was lost to us forever.

This statement has been made by me under oath, and is true in every respect.

Signed.	Nai Sing Kham Thongbai.
Witness. Signed.	Nai Chalaw Sompetch.
District Officer.	Huey Luk.
English translation by me:-	Signed, Nai Parn Swasdi.
	Schoolmaster, Chiengmai.

*   *   *

BLOOD RELATIONS

Dr. Sawang Worathai was more English than Thai. At the age of twelve, his parents had sent him to England, and he did not return to Thailand until he was a young man of twenty-eight. In that long interval he had attended a famous public school, and acquired the right, along with so many other distinguished men, to put the letters "O.A." after his name. But that worthy "O.A." was swamped by the vast array of letters indicating almost every medical and surgical degree which London and Edinburgh have it in their power to bestow.

Soon after his return to Thailand, Dr. Sawang was sent to Chiengmai to take charge of the surgical work at the Mengrai Hospital in that city. Away there in the North, he soon found that, though his medical colleagues shared his modern and rationalistic opinions, many of his neighbours still clung to the beliefs and superstitions of bygone days. Being of a good-natured and tolerant disposition, he regarded the old-fashioned beliefs of his northern friends with amused indifference — until he met Nang Lamai Potaram.

Nang Lamai was a young widow of twenty-four. She had been married at the age of seventeen to an Army Lieutenant, who was killed only a year later in the Korean war. She was left with one small boy, named Boon Lert, who was four years old when Dr. Sawang arrived in Chiengmai. Nang Lamai's personal attractions were considerable, and she had received many offers of marriage, but she had remained faithful to the memory of her dead husband, and had devoted herself to the task of bringing up her little boy. She lived with her old mother in a roomy house close to the Mengrai Hospital. Having several rooms to spare, Nang Lamai and her mother were in the habit of taking in some of the doctors and other members of the hospital staff as boarders.

Soon after his arrival at Chiengmai, Dr. Sawang went to board in the house of Nang Lamai and her mother. They looked after him very well, gave him excellent food, and before long a warm friendship sprang up between the smart young doctor and the pretty widow.

As the months passed by, Sawang found himself growing more and more attached to Lamai and her sturdy little son. But one thing worried him. Lamai appeared to him to be immersed in every possible kind of superstition. She was afraid of ghosts, and constantly consulted astrologers and mediums even in regard to the most trivial matters. She would not go to have her hair permed, or give a dose of medicine to her little boy, without first taking advice as to whether it was a lucky day or not. Sawang did his best to persuade her that all her cherished beliefs were baseless and useless, but she laughed at him, and said:— "In Chiengmai we all believe in things like this. I am too old to change; and what harm does it do, anyhow?"

One evening, Sawang happened to be alone in Lamais' sitting-room with her little son Boon Lert. As he looked at the little boy, a feeling of strong affection came over him. He lifted the child onto his knee, and said:— "You are a fine, strong little chap. When you grow up, I am sure you will be a brave and noble man, like your father." At that moment, Lamai entered the room. Sawang heard her give a gasp of horror, and when he looked up, he saw that her face was drawn and pale.

"How can you talk to my child like that?" she exclaimed. "Do you not understand that you are sure to bring some rightful misfortune upon him by saying things of that sort?"

Sawang tried to reassure her, telling her that in England people like to have their children praised and admired, but she paid no attention. "We are not in England," she protested, "we are in Chiengmai. Here you will only bring us trouble and sorrow with your foreign ways and ideas. I cannot allow you to stay in this house any longer. Please pack your things and go away as soon as possible."

Argument was of no avail. Sawang had trampled underfoot two of the most cherished superstitions of Northern Thailand. He had spoken of a small child in terms of praise, and he had made a hopeful prognostication concerning its future. Lamai's heart was filled with the direst forebodings, and she felt that she never wished to see Sawang again.

Sorrowfully, Sawang collected his belongings, and went away to stay with a friend in the city.

A few days later, little Boon Lert was playing in the front garden of his mother's house when a kitten came through the open gate. He ran to catch it, but it fled away from him back into the street. He had been told again and again never to go out through the gate, but in the excitement of chasing the kitten the little fellow forgot all the warnings he had received, and followed it into the road. A motor samlor was coming along, trying to overtake another. Everything happened in a moment. There was a screeching of brakes, a lot of shouting, a rush of onlookers into the middle of the road. There lay poor Boon Lert, limp and unconscious, and bleeding, bleeding terribly. Lamai, hearing the noise, ran out too. Then she saw her child lying on the road in a pool of blood. However, she did not entirely lose her head. She quickly picked him up in her arms, and ran, ran madly to the hospital close by. There she laid him on the front step, and fainted away.

When she came to, she found herself lying in a private ward of the hospital. A nurse was washing away the blood which had covered her from head to foot.

"Where is my child?" she asked. "Take me to him, take me to him at once."

"Lie still, my dear," said the nurse, "your little boy is being well looked after. He is in the hands of Dr. Tawi Manorom, and everything possible is being done for him."

"But he was bleeding so terribly! He was bleeding to death! Take me to him!"

"Dr. Tawi has stopped the bleeding," answered the nurse, "and he has every hope of saving his life. Lie quietly here and do not try to interfere. You will only worry the doctors. Trust to them, and everything will be all right."

With difficulty Lamai controlled herself, and waited for about half an hour. Then the door opened, and Dr. Tawi came in. He was the Superintendent of the hospital — an elderly grey-haired man, whom she knew well. As soon as she saw his face, hope awoke in her heart.

"Cheer up, Nang Lamai," said the old doctor. "Your little son will not die. He has broken his left arm, and one of his arteries was damaged, which caused all that terrible bleeding. But we have set his arm, and have carried out a transfusion of blood. He will recover and be as strong as ever. In a month from now, all you will see to remind you of the accident will be a small scar on his left arm."

"Transfusion!" exclaimed Lamai. "That means putting somebody's blood into his veins, does it not? Was it another little boy's blood? How wonderful!"

"No," answered Dr. Tawi. "It was the blood of a strong young man. Have no fear. Everything will be all right. Come along with me now, and you shall see your son. He is sleeping peacefully."

"But, doctor, you must tell me first the name of the young man who gave his blood to save my child. I must thank him."

"I have made it a rule not to tell my patients or their relatives the names of blood donors in cases like this," answered Dr. Tawi. "So it must remain a secret. Now come along with me, and you shall see your son. Tomorrow I will hand him over to the care of Dr. Sawang, so he will be in good hands, and you need have no fear."

"Dr. Sawang," exclaimed Lamai. "I would rather he had nothing to do with my little boy. I do not trust him. He used to be my friend, but I do not like him any more. I believe it was through something he said that this terrible accident took place."

"How can you talk so foolishly, Nang Lamai?" said the old doctor. "It is ridiculous to say that Dr. Sawang was in any way responsible for the accident, whatever he may have said. Far from it! If you are going to worry your head with such absurd fancies, maybe I must make an exception to my general rule, and tell you that Dr. Sawang is the man who gave his blood for transfusion into little Boon Lert's veins. He it is who has saved the life of your son. But for him, it is quite certain that the little fellow would be lying dead at this moment."

Lamai turned pale. "I am a wicked, black-hearted woman," she cried. "But you have opened my eyes to the truth, and I will never let any foolish fancies mislead me again. Take me at once to see Dr. Sawang, that I may thank him. Take me even before I see Boon Lert."

"Dr. Sawang has gone home to lie down and rest," said Dr. Tawi. "We generally like a blood donor to do this for a few hours. But he will be all right tomorrow, and you shall see him and thank him if you thank it right to do so."

Then Lamai went with Dr. Tawi to see her son. Boon Lert was lying asleep. All traces of blood had been washed away. His left arm was in a splint, but otherwise he appeared to have nothing wrong with him. His colour was good, and he was breathing regularly.

Lamai could hardly wait until the next morning. At an early hour she set forth on her bicycle for Sawang's lodging.

Running up the steps, she met him coming out on his way to the hospital to see Boon Lert.

"Forgive me, forgive me," she cried, tears running down her face. "I am a wicked, ungrateful woman. I was a fool to set up my ignorant ideas against your knowledge and experience. You, and you alone, have saved the life of my child. You have risked your life by giving your own life-blood to flow in his veins. Now he is your son, more truly even than he is mine, more even than he is the son of my former dear husband. I want to give him to you to keep for ever, if you will take him."

"There is nothing to forgive," replied Sawang, "and nothing to thank me for. I ran no risk by giving a little blood to save our dear Boon Lert. Many men have given blood again and again to save others, and have suffered no ill effects. I do not blame you for having been angry with me. It was foolish of me to despise the ancient beliefs of you and my other Northern neighbours. Old ideas cannot be discarded in a moment."

Then he took Lamai gently by the hand, and said:— "I am truly grateful to you for offering to entrust your little son to me. I love him, and will gladly take him to keep and look after, and will be like a true and loving father to him. But I can only do this on one condition. You must come too! I love you as much as I love your child, and I want you both. Take pity on me, and do not let me be a lonely bachelor any longer. I promise you that from now on I will always say that Boon Lert is a horrid, ugly little brat, and destined to come to a bad end!"

"Do not tease me and make fun of me, dear Sawang," said Lamai. "I have finished with all those foolish ideas for ever. Take us both, me and my son. We shall be the happiest family in all Thailand, and we will bring up Boon Lert to be a great and learned doctor, for he is a blood relation of the cleverest doctor and the kindest man in the whole world."

THE TWO CORPORALS

Army Corporal Lerm and Police Corporal Serm had been buddies since the days when they crawled about on all fours At school they had worked and played side by side. Both played football, both collected stamps, and both had a liking for pretty maidens. Lerm joined the Army and Serm the Police on the same day. Now, at the age of twenty-four, both of them were full-fledged Corporals. All their neighbours and friends in their native village near Chiengmai called them "The twins." Until the month of March in the year of the Buddhist Era 2504, they had never disagreed about anything.

But in that fatal month of March, their habit of agreement carried them too far. They both agreed that Nangsao Bua Kiow was the most beautiful girl in the whole world. She really was a very pretty girl, so attractive, indeed, that she had been runner-up in a competition for the title of "Miss Chiengmai."

But though our two young heroes agreed in admiring this charming maiden, they disagreed (for the first time in their lives) on a very important point. They failed to see eye to eye on the question of finding a suitable husband for her; each of them was convinced that he himself, and not his dear buddy, was the right man to occupy that enviable position.

Within a few weeks, Lerm and Serm began to regard one another with feelings of hatred. When Lerm went to visit Bua Kiow one evening, taking with him his guitar, and hoping to entrance her with his sweet music, he was disgusted to find Serm serenading her with his mouth organ. A few evenings later, Serm, in his turn, was terribly upset, on arriving at his charmer's house, to find her executing a few dance steps to the music of Larm's guitar.

At last Lerm felt he could bear it no longer. He sought out an old man of the village, named Pu Neuk, who had the reputation of being a magician, and asked him whether it would be possible, by some occult art, to remove his rival from his path.

51

"My son," said Pu Neuk, "in a matter like this, half-measures are useless. I could very easily cause Corporal Serm to fall seriously ill, but that would only arouse a sympathetic interest in the heart of the young lady you admire. The only possible course is the complete removal of your antagonist."

Jealousy had so poisoned Lerm's mind that he replied:— "I don't care what you do, Grandfather. Remove Corporal Serm from my path, and I will reward you handsomely."

The old wizard then produced from his box of magic gadgets a lump of wax. From this he rapidly made a little figure of a man. It was beautifully sculptured, perfect in every respect, even down to its tiny toes and fingers. Then the magician wove a little basket of twigs, in which he laid the miniature man.

"Now," said he, handing a sharp needle to Lerm, "take this needle, and pierce the wax image in the head, the heart, or the stomach. If you pierce its heart, Corporal Serm will have a fit and die suddenly; transfix its head, and he will go mad and jump over a precipice; jab it in the stomach, and he will waste away with an attack of dysentery. After you have pierced the image, take it along at night and lay it under your rival's house, and you will have no cause to worry about him any more."

Lerm took the needle and held it poised over the little image, but he could not bring himself to the point of piercing it in the head, the heart, or the stomach. He remembered all the happy times he and Serm had spent together, and he said to himself:— "I cannot kill him. That would be too wicked. I will make him lame, and Bua Kiow will not want to be burdened with a cripple. So here goes!" So saying, he pierced the leg of the wax image with the needle.

Late that same night, Lerm went along and secretly laid the little image on the earth underneath the flooring of Serm's house.

During all the rest of the night, he was tormented by feelings of doubt and anxiety. Soon after dawn, he mounted his bicycle and set forth for Serm's dwelling to find out what had happened. He had hardly started out when a dog suddenly ran across his path. He swerved, wobbled, and fell sprawling to the earth. When he got up, he found that he had sprained his right knee. Cycling was impossible, so he sat down by the wayside to wait for a lift from some passing vehicle.

A few moments later, along came Corporal Serm, riding his bicycle. He was holding the handle-bar with his left hand, and had his right arm in a sling. He dismounted and came to Lerm.

"What is the matter?" he asked. "Are you hurt?"

Lerm looked at the face of his old friend, and instantly felt deeply grieved and repentant, when he thought of the injury he had planned to do him.

"Dear brother Serm," he said, "I ran over a dog, and seem to have sprained my right knee. It is very painful. But I am sure that this is a punishment which I have brought upon myself by my frightful wickedness. I had actually planned, by means of a wax image made for me by that villainous old ruffian Pu Neuk, to try to kill you. But I could not bring myself to do this, by piercing the image in a vital part, so I pierced its leg, intending to make you lame. My evil design has now recoiled upon me, and now I have sprained my own knee, and no doubt shall be lame for the rest of my life. And serve me right, too!"

When he heard these words, Corporal Serm shed tears, and said:— "Dear brother Lerm, I am as bad as you. I, too, went to that horrible old scoundrel, and he made one of his vile wax images for me to pierce. But like you, I could not bring myself to pierce it in a vital spot, so I jabbed it in the right arm. And here am I now with my own right arm badly sprained, for I fell down-stairs early this morning and ran my arm against the gate-post. I am sure it is permanently injured, and I shall have to resign from the Police. And just think! We two dear old buddies had come to hate each other on account of a girl!! And what a girl!!! Late last night I heard that she had run away to Bangkok with that rich old Chinese who runs a sugar-mill near her house. He has two other wives already. We have quarrelled and tried to injure each other for the sake of a girl who is no better than a tart!"

"What an escape we have had!" exclaimed Lerm. "I cannot think why either of us ever bothered to look at her at

53

all. Why, she is not even pretty! She has a cast in her left eye, and her face is all pimply."

"Absolutely true," agreed Serm. "Moreover, she has a limp, and her breath smells of onions."

"Garlic!" corrected Serm. "But I do not intend to worry my mind about her for another moment. I know a girl far prettier than Bua Kiow, and I am sure she likes me."

"Same here," said Lerm. "But I do hope it is not the same girl! That would be terrible; we should be back again where we started. What is the first letter of your new girl's name?"

"M," answered Serm.

"Hooray," shouted Lerm. "Mine begins with L. Everything is perfect. We will have a double wedding. Come along now. We will go to see a doctor, and no doubt he will be able to fix us up in no time. We have confessed our sin to one another, and are pure in heart, so we are sure to recover quickly. But what shall we do to that wicked old devil, Pu Neuk? Do you realise that the old brute actually plotted to murder both of us?"

"So he did!" replied Serm. "Just wait till we've got back the full use of our arms and legs, and we'll go along and give him a lesson he won't forget it a hurry!"

*   *   *

LOBINSON CLUSOE

Sompongs Borapetch of Muang Lerm was a young man who possessed a great stock of bounce and self-confidence. At the age of twenty-five he found himself the owner of two motor-buses and a garage, with a comfortable flat above it. He was a bachelor, though hardly a celibate. His good looks appealed to the girls, and his strength and success in business gained him the respect of his men friends. He had not a care in the world.

Then misfortune struck, and struck hard. A faulty electric connection, a short circuit, a handy can of petrol, and in less than half an hour the whole world of Sompongs was changed. His garage and his buses had gone up in smoke, together with all his savings, which he kept in a wooden box under his bed. From being a prosperous man, he found himself a pauper. All he owned in the world was a shirt, a pair of trousers, a pair of shoes and a wrist-watch. To add to his load of misery, a pretty girl, on whom he had long had his eye, and whom he had even thought of marrying, had gone off with another fellow!

A man who has known nothing but success usually bears loss and trouble badly. It was so with Sompongs. On the afternoon following the day of the fire which had brought him to ruin, he set forth alone from the city, bearing in his hand a small sack and a piece of rope. The river Me Lerm was in flood, and he made slow progress, wading through the water along the river bank, until he came to a place where he thought he would be safe from interference. Then he picked up several of the largest stones he could find, put them into the sack, and was about to tie the rope round his waist and jump into the water. But at that moment he saw a little black dog, yapping frantically, being borne away helpless by the swollen waters of the river.

"I am tired of life," thought Sompongs, "but that little dog is not. It wants to live. I will do one good deed before I die."

Without further hesitation, Sompongs threw down his sack of stones, plunged into the river, and in a few strokes reached the little dog. He was a powerful swimmer, but with his left hand grasping the dog, he found himself unable to contend against the current, which was set in a direction away from the bank. "No help for it," he thought, "I must simply keep afloat and see where the current decides to land us." By this time, all idea of suicide had vanished from his mind. He was governed only by the instinct to keep afloat and to save the little dog.

The river below Muang Lerm is full of islands. The flooded waters bore Sompongs helpless past three of these;

then, as he was being carried past a fourth island, he managed, by a supreme effort, to reach the shore.

The danger he had just passed through, and the excitement of his struggle with the raging river, had brought back a good deal of Sompongs' self-assurance and confidence. "Well," said he to himself, "here I am, marooned on a desert island, just like that Englishman I read about in the *Thai Phab* Magazine. Lobinson Clusoe, his name was. (Like most of the people in Northern Thailand, Sompongs had no use at all for the letter *R*.) I am Lobinson Clusoe the Second. What is more, though I have no black man named Fliday to look after me, I have a little black dog, and I shall call him Fliday. Come along, Fliday, and we will explore our island."

The exploration did not take long. The island, in normal times, may have been about two hundred yards long, but only some fifty yards of it were now above water. This small area formed part of a vegetable garden, in which were growing a few haricot beans, some sweet potatoes, and half a dozen cauliflowers. The greater part of the garden had been swept away. There was also a small lamyai tree, near which stood a tiny bamboo hut. "Splendid," exclaimed Sompongs, "I shall not have to build myself a hut, as the other Lobinson did. Come along, Fliday, we will have a look inside."

It was a miserable little hut, evidently used by the owner's watchman. It consisted only of one small room, with a tiny verandah outside, one corner of which was set aside for cooking. In the room was a rough mattress, a hard and dirty pillow, and a torn blanket. But, best of all, there was a box of matches and a small bag containing some rice, and half a dried fish.

"Never mind if we have to stay here for a week, Fliday," said Sompongs, "we have rice, plenty of vegetables, and a delicious bit of dried fish. What a pity it is I am such a poor cook."

Sompongs decided that the owner of the island, or his watchman, had probably gone over in the morning to the nearest village to buy food, but had not ventured to recross the river, as the water had risen several feet since morning, and the current had increased in speed and fury. "However," he thought, "if he knows that a man is marooned here, maybe

56

he will make an effort to bring his boat across. Here is a long bamboo. I will stick it up, hoist my shirt on it, and see what happens."

He had just begun to dig a hole in which to insert the bamboo, when he saw a log floating down the river. Clinging to it were two people, apparently a man and a woman. Sompongs quickly realised that the current would carry the log and its passengers away past the island unless he did something about it. He therefore held out the end of the bamboo towards the log, calling out:— "Grab the end of the bamboo! Quick, or you will be swept past!"

The man on the log, who appeared to be in a state of collapse, did nothing, but the woman seized the end of the bamboo, and Sompongs managed to pull the log to the shore. The impact caused the man to fall into the water. He sank at once, but Sompongs plunged in after him, and succeeded in dragging him ashore.

Sompongs had, when at school, been a boy scout, and had some idea of first aid to the semi-drowned. He rolled his water-logged visitor, who proved to be a rather stout Chinese, over on his face, and with a little vigorous arm exercise soon succeeded in bringing him back to consciousness. Then he had a good look at his other visitor. She was a girl of about twenty, and her attractions were such that Sompongs instantly gave up his plan of hoisting his shirt to attract possible assistance from the mainland.

Addressing the Chinese, Sompongs said:— "Do you know that you sank seven times under the water, and that it was only with immense difficulty, and at imminent risk to my own life, that I succeeded in bringing you ashore? Then, with the valuable assistance of this young lady, (do not interrupt or argue, I beg of you, my dear) I managed to restore you to consciousness. You were very fortunate to meet a man of strength, courage and resourcefulness, and a young lady of quick intelligence and skilful at first aid; if I and this young lady had been ordinary people, you would have been a dead man."

"Now," he continued, "we will introduce ourselves. "My name is Lobinson Clusoe, and this is my dog Fliday. I am one of the best motor mechanics and drivers in Thailand, can

57

box and play football, perform on the violin and guitar, and sing most beautifully. The only thing I cannot do well is to cook. Tell me, my dear young lady, can you cook? As we are likely to spend a night, or maybe a week, on this island, the question is an important one."

"My name is Amporn Intawongs," said the pretty girl, "and I am by profession a teacher of cookery and household management. Give me anything which is capable of being cooked, and I will cook it for you."

"Magnificent," exclaimed Sompongs, "I have plenty of excellent food for you to grapple with; rice, beans, potatoes, and delicious dried fish. As for household management, the only house on this island does not call for much management; but you can try. And now, Sir," he continued, addressing the fat Chinese, "tell us all about yourself, and what you can do to help."

"My name is Kim Lok Cheng," replied the fat man. "I am a garage proprietor, and own four buses and five cars. I cannot cook or do household management, nor can I swim, or play football, or twang a guitar, but I assure you that I will do all I can for you in other ways. I fully realise that but for you, Sir, and you, Miss, I would not have been alive at this moment."

"But tell me this," enquired Sompongs, "what were you doing travelling about on a log with this young lady?"

"This young lady and I are strangers to one another," answered Lok Cheng. "We happened to be crossing the river in the ferry-boat, when a log struck the boat. We were close to the shore, and all the other passengers swam to safety. Only I and this young lady, who could not swim, clung to the log. Had you not been on this island, and had you not dragged us to safety, we were lost."

"But why did you, a non-swimmer, want to cross the river by ferry at such a dangerous time?" asked Sompongs.

"As you know, the bridge is down," said Lok Cheng, "and I was on my way to the Telegraph Office to send off a wire to engage a new Manager for my garage. My old Manager's father has just died suddenly, and he and his wife have been called down to Bangkok to take over the family business."

"Lucky man!" cried Sompongs. "If that log had not hit the ferry-boat, you would have sent off a wire to engage some wretched, second-rate, incompetent fellow to take charge of your garage; you would no doubt have ended by being completely ruined. As it is, you have been cast onto this beautiful little island, where you have met Lobinson Clusoe, who is a first-class mechanic and a skilful driver — just the very man you need!"

"But I rather wanted a married man, whose wife could cook for the staff," objected Lok Cheng.

"That will be quite all right." replied Sompongs. "True, I am a bachelor at the moment, but I intend to get married almost at once. The girl I have in mind is a good cook — she has actually taught cookery and household management; just the sort of girl you need! But let us not talk any more just now. We are all three wet and cold. There are plenty of old bamboos near that hut. Let us make a big fire and dry ourselves. After that, we will sample Miss Amporn's cookery."

So they lit a great bonfire, and soon began to feel much more cheerful and full of life. When they were thoroughly warmed up, Amporn put the piece of dried fish, together with a cauliflower, some beans, and a few sweet potatoes into a pot, and produced a sort of ragout. They had no salt, so it tasted a bit insipid, but they were all hungry, and the two men pronounced it excellent, and complimented Amporn on her skill. Fliday ate as much as any of them.

"You see, Towkay," said Sompongs, "all your difficulties are at an end. As soon as we are rescued from this island, Miss Amporn and I will get married, and you will then have a thoroughly competent man and wife, ready to start work at once. As for terms, we will accept the same pay as you gave to our predecessors, plus thirty per cent extra for having saved your life. I feel sure you will not try to argue or raise difficulties. That would be quite unworthy of you!"

"But how about me?" cried Amporn. "What makes you suppose that I would be willing to marry you? Why, we have only known each other for a couple of hours! The idea is ridiculous!"

"What I said to the Towkay about *arguing* applies equally to you, my dear," said Sompongs. "It is a very bad habit, which I hope you will try to avoid after we are married. But we will talk over this again in the morning. Night is coming on, we have had a strenuous day, and we all need some sleep. You, my dear girl, shall sleep in the little room, and the Towkay and I on the verandah of the hut. I will sleep, with my dog Fliday, close to your door, to guard you from all danger."

"How about letting the Towkay sleep near the door?" asked Amporn. "He is a much older man than you, so perhaps it would be more suitable."

"Suitable, indeed!" exclaimed Sompongs, "You do not know these rich Chinese so well as I do. They all have at least four wives, and are always on the look-out for a few more. I am a respectable young bachelor, of the highest moral character. No more argument! I and my dog Fliday will sleep outside your door to guard you."

*   *   *

Next morning, when the first streaks of dawn began to spread across the sky, an observer, had there been one there, would have noticed that Lok Cheng was sleeping all alone on the verandah of the hut, snoring lustily. A few minutes later, he would have seen the bamboo door of the little room open very quietly and gently; then he would have observed the figure of Lobinson Clusoe Sompongs emerging somewhat stealthily from the room.

Advancing to the sleeping Chinese, Sompongs shook him vigorously, and called out:— "Wake up, wake up, Towkay! The river has fallen several feet in the night. We shall have the owner of the island coming across in his boat any moment. We must be ready to receive him properly. I wish I had a comb and a piece of scented soap."

Then he knocked, or rather scratched, on the door of the little room. "Get up, get up, Miss Amporn," he cried, "we must all be ready to receive the proprietor of the island."

When Amporn appeared, he said:— "Good morning, my dear; I hope you slept well, with me and my faithful dog Fliday guarding your door. And I hope that you have made up your mind to marry me, and do not intend to go on arguing about it."

60

"I am ready to marry you any day that suits you, Lobinson Clusoe," said Amporn, "and I will never argue with you again as long as I live. I have found by experience that it is quite useless to do so — mere waste of time and breath."

"So that's settled!" said Sompongs. "And now I see our life as islanders is at an end, and our new life is about to begin."

Soon the little boat reached the island, and a young man of about the same age as Sompongs stepped out. Sompongs, advancing with outstretched hand, greeted him as follows:—

"Good morning, Sir; we beg you to forgive us for occupying your island and your watchman's hut; also for eating your rice, some of your vegetables, and your delicious bit of dried fish. But we were helpless refugees, cast ashore by the waters of the flood. My name is Lobinson Clusoe. I am Manager and Chief Mechanic of a garage owned by this gentleman, Towkay Kim Lok Cheng. This young lady, Miss Amporn Intawongs, is engaged to marry me, and is to be head cook and manageress for the garage staff."

"My name is Sawat Phakdi," said the new arrival. "I own this island and garden — or what remains of it after the flood. I am glad you three people were able to take shelter here and to find a little food to eat. If there is anything more I can do for you, let me know."

"It is very kind of you to say that," said Sompongs. "As a matter of fact, I have two favours I would like to ask of you. Firstly, I trust you will take us all across the river in your boat, if there is room enough. Then, I must explain, Miss Amporn and I have arranged to get married this morning. Towkay Lok Cheng will lend us his smartest car, and will drive us to the District Office to register our marriage. He will be one of our witnesses. I trust you will come with us to be the second witness. This would be very fitting, as we first met on your island."

"I will gladly do that," answered Sawat, "and what is more, I would be honoured if you would all come back, after the ceremony, to my house on the opposite bank, and let my wife and myself put up a hurried wedding breakfast for you, with a few bottles of Mekong whisky."

"Before we actually set out for the District Office," said Amporn, "there is one little matter I want to ask about, with

61

no intention of trying to argue. What is your real name? You forgot to tell me."

"So I did!" exclaimed Sompongs. "My name is Sompongs Borapetch, but I would rather you called me Lobinson Clusoe. That name will always remind me of the night I spent, with my dog Fliday, sleeping on guard outside your bedroom door. But there is still one more point to be considered. I have no other clothes except the dirty shirt and trousers you see me wearing now; in fact, these are the only property I own in the world, except my wrist-watch and my dog Fliday. While Miss Amporn goes home to smarten herself up, I must do a little shopping. I shall have to buy a new shirt, a decent suit, and a pair of presentable shoes. I thought also that a scarlet beret would brighten up my appearance a bit. No doubt, Towkay, you will advance me a few hundred bahts to purchase my wedding outfit."

"Nobody shall buy your wedding outfit but me," exclaimed Amporn. "I have six hundred bahts with me, safe in a little waterproof bag. I will not allow anyone else to pay for Lobinson Clusoe's new clothes."

"That's the right sort of wife for me!" cried Sompongs "So now everything's settled. No need to wait here any longer. Farewell, beautiful little island! Goodbye, lovely little hut! Quick march! Away we go! All aboard! Come along, Fliday!"

And little Fliday wagged his tail and braked.

THE STONE MONKEY

"Another confounded globe-trotter!" exclaimed Philip Grant in disgust, flinging down the telegram just received from his head office in Bangkok. "This makes the fourth this month! Mr. Bertram Bloom, Member of Parliament for Billsbury. I'm certain he is one of the aggressive type."

Grant was the local representative at Wieng Muan, in Northern Thailand, for the International Liquid Fuel Syndicate, Limited. Unfortunately for him, Wieng Muan is situated on the banks of the only large lake in Thailand, and is also the site of a very celebrated Buddhist temple. It thus often happened that globe-trotters who wanted to see something of Northern Thailand were advised to visit Wieng Muan. Grant was the only European in the place, and so it usually fell to his lot to pilot the visitors around the city — a job he detested.

There are many kinds of globe-trotters, but most of them, in Grant's opinion, fell into one of two categories. The earnest ones, who wanted to photograph everything they saw from seventeen angles and to spend hours taking down voluminous notes, and the boisterous ones, who blustered about the place making personal remarks about everyone they met, under the delusion that nobody East of Gibraltar could speak English, and who seemed to go out of their way to offend the feelings of the Thai people.

"I feel certain that Bertram Bloom is a boisterous bounder," said Grant to himself.

A few days later the distinguished politician arrived, and Grant's worst fears were at once confirmed. Mr. Bloom was a big, stout man, with a red face and a loud voice, who swaggered around as though he owned the earth. If he went to buy anything in a shop, he chucked the wares about, describing them as trash and rubbish, and stigmatised the shop-keeper as a thief and robber. In a restaurant he would thrust the food away, calling it filthy muck, shout at the servants, and give infinitesimal tips.

When Grant was asked to take his unwelcome guest to see the great temple, his heart sank. However, he felt he had to go through with it, so off they went.

The main temple building had a figure of a Thai heraldic lion on each side. The doors were closed, so Grant suggested that they should go round to the side of the building and enter by one of the smaller doors. The steps of the side door were flanked by two short pillars. On top of the right-hand pillar squatted the stone figure of a monkey. The left-hand pillar was bare. An elderly Buddhist priest was standing in front of the monkey-less pillar.

"Look at that," said Mr. Bloom in his would-be facetious way, pointing his finger at the old man; "they have lost one of their monkeys; they ought to put that old blighter there

63

to take its place. I'm damned if he isn't uglier than the stone monkey!"

"Don't point your finger at him," angrily exclaimed Grant. "Thai people hate being pointed at. And, anyhow, that priest is an elderly man, and accustomed to being treated with respect. Remember, I live in this town, and it is important for me to remain on good terms with the people here."

Then, turning to the old priest, he said:— "Reverend Father, please do not be offended. This gentleman is a stranger, and does not understand Thai customs."

Speaking in perfect English, the old man replied:— "I am not offended with you, Nai. I know you well by name, and know how highly you are respected by everybody here. As for your friend, he is likely to injure himself more than me by behaving in a vulgar manner."

"You speak English very well," said Grant in surprise, "where did you learn it?"

"My father was formerly Thai Minister in London," replied the old man. "I was born and educated in England; but no doubt I have changed a good deal since the time when Queen Victoria was kind enough to refer to me as a 'little darling."

"Come on," said Mr. Bloom angrily, "let's go up and have a look at the place."

Grant sat down on the steps of the temple and started to take off his shoes. Mr. Bloom snorted.

"What's the use of that," he asked. "What's in there, anyhow, but a great big plated idol?"

Grant managed with difficulty to control his temper, and replied:— "Do as you like. In Thailand, people are very tolerant towards foreigners who visit their temples. In Burma, you would be in for a very unpleasant time if you went into a temple with your shoes on. As for me, I prefer to leave my shoes on the steps. But now, come on, and let's get the business finished."

So saying, he walked up the steps and went into the temple, with Mr. Bloom close behind him.

"Lord, how dark it is," exclaimed the M.P. "I can't see a blooming thing. Can't we get Queen Victoria's little darling to open a couple of windows for us?"

64

"I do not feel like asking that old priest to do anything for us, after what happened just now," answered Grant, "but just stand here a minute, and I will go across and open a window on the other side."

Suiting the action to the words, he walked across the temple, opened a window on the opposite side, and returned.

Mr. Bloom was nowhere to be seen. He had apparently changed his mind about his shoes, for they, with his socks inside them, were to be seen close to the door through which their owner had entered, but he himself had vanished

Then Grant observed with amazement that all Mr. Bloom's clothes and belongings were lying about on the floor of the temple — his shirt, trousers, underpants, belt, tie and wristlet watch. Grant began to gather them up, and as he did so, he noticed a very strange fact — none of the garments which possessed buttons had had the buttons unfastened. It seemed as though Mr. Bloom had not taken them off, but had been liquified or disintegrated out of them!

Nothing was missing. Mr. Bloom's pocket-book, containing a fairly large amount of money, was in the hip pocket of his trousers.

Carrying the clothes and shoes, Grant hurried out to the top of the steps. The old priest was still standing where they had left him only a few minutes earlier.

"Reverend Father," enquired Grant, "did the gentleman who went into the temple with me just now come out again? I cannot see him in the temple, but all his clothes were there, lying on the floor. I have them all here."

"I have seen nobody come out since you both went in," replied the old man, "and all the other doors of the building are shut. How could he have come out wearing no clothes?"

Then a curious circumstance attracted Grant's attention. Whereas, when he entered the temple, there had only been one stone monkey at the foot of the steps, there were now two, one on each side.

"Reverend Father," he exclaimed, "just now there was only one stone monkey here — that one, to the right of the steps. Now there are two. Why is this?"

"One of the monkeys was damaged, and had been sent out to be repaired," said the old priest. "The mason brought

....there had been only one stone monkey at the foot of the steps, there were now two, one on each side.

it back while you were in the temple. But let us not waste valuable time talking about stone monkeys, when we have the important matter of your friend's disappearance to consider. I advise you to go at once to the Police Station and make a report on the matter."

So off went Grant to the Police Station. In a very short time, a Police Lieutenant and four constables were on the spot. All the temple buildings and precincts were thoroughly searched, the well sounded, and everyone around the place examined and cross-examined for hours. But no trace could be found of the missing M.P.

A few days later, after dozens of telegrams had passed between London and Bangkok, a special investigator was sent up from the capital to Wieng Muan. Every man, woman and child in the town was interrrogated, every house was searched, but all without even the most meagre result. Mr. Bertram Bloom, Member of Parliament for Billsbury, had completely vanished. Nor has anything ever been heard of him from that day to this.

During the investigation, Grant somewhat diffidently asked the Police Officer from Bangkok whether he had heard of the curious coinsidence of one of the stone monkeys near the temple door, which had been missing when Mr. Bloom entered the temple, having been replaced. The Police Officer, however, showed some impatience, and replied, more or less as the old priest had done:—

"I am extremely busy investigating a matter of international importance, the disappearance in this town of a Member of the British Parliament. Why do you want to talk to me about stone monkeys, which cannot possibly have anything to do with the case?"

This reply was so obviously correct and reasonable that Grant hardly felt justified in pursuing the matter any further.

So there the case rests — an unsolved mystery. But every few weeks, Grant goes along to the great temple and gazes earnestly at the two stone monkeys, especially the one on the left-hand side of the steps.

"I wonder," he says to himself, "I wonder —." And then he calls to mind rather a hackneyed quotation from Hamlet, Act I, Scene 4.

THE GANGSTER

"Please, please, brother Kampan, take me with you to-night. I want to be one of the White Eagles, too."

"You are too young, Boon Mee, and too small. You are only sixteen. We White Eagles are not a schoolboy gang. We go in for dangerous work. We have no member under seventeen."

"Please, please, big brother, tell them I am seventeen. I want so much to be a White Eagle, like you."

Kampan, aged nineteen, was by day a bus driver, earning good pay. By night he was a "gangster." He was one of the White Eagles, a teenager gang which, with several others, infested the district of Chiengmai, in Northern Thailand. What had induced him to join a gang it is difficult to say. Love of excitement, a desire to "show off" to other lads of the village, maybe just sheer "cussedness."

The two brothers lived with their mother, Nang Waen, a widow, in a village some miles from the city. They were not poor people. They owned a good house, a rice-field and two buffaloes. Nang Waen ran a market stall, Kampan was well paid by the local bus Company, and Boon Mee, or the "Little One," as his mother called him, did very well growing and selling cabbages and cauliflowers.

Boon Mee had a sports bicycle, a smart wristlet watch, and a small radio set. But he was not satisfied. He found life dull and unromantic. He wanted to be a brave hero, such as he imagined his elder brother to be. His one ambition was to become a member of the White Eagle gang.

Kampan did not suffer any pangs of conscience on account of his association with a gang whose activities were at best a nuisance, and at times criminal. But he fell somehow that he did not want his brother, the "Little One," to follow in his footsteps.

However, constant dripping wears away even a stone, so at last Kampan gave in.

"All right," said he, "the White Eagles have a great plan for tomorrow night, and I will take you with me. Forty of us intend to carry out a raid at the fair which is being held at the temple of Dawn, in Samrit village, five miles away. We will knock over all the stalls, beat up anyone who opposes us, and in the confusion pinch any money or portable property which is lying handy. The whole job will not take more than five minutes, and we shall terrorise the whole population of the village."

"But you must be properly dressed. No true White Eagle would dream, when out on a raid, of wearing the sort of clothes you have on. Come along with me now, and we will see about providing you with a proper outfit."

So off they went to a back lane in the city. There they found a small tailor's shop, at which they bought a shirt with green, yellow and blue, stripes, a pair of black trousers as tight as sausage-skins, a white plastic hat and a pair of large black goggles. Rigged out in these, wearing a bit of red rag round the little finger of his left hand, and with his watch on his right wrist, Kampan felt himself to be a true White Eagle.

Then the two brothers visited a barber, where our budding gangster had his hair beautifully and expensively "permed," with a saucy curl trained to dangle down on each side of his face. In theory, these curls should have intertwined with his sideburns; but, alas! he had none.

Boon Mee now believed himself to be a real desperado, capable of tackling any policeman up to, and including the rank of Major, or of fighting any other gangster — even Duang Keow, the leader of the Water-Rats, a tough old veteran of twenty-two.

The next evening at eight o'clock the two brothers set out on their bicycles for Samrit village. The raid had been carefully planned. The White Eagles had been divided into five parties of eight men each. They were to ride out to the village, and to leave their bicycles in five different places, all of them near the temple of Dawn, where the fair was being held. The leader was to blow a whistle, whereupon the whole gang, all wearing black goggles, was to converge upon the temple, upset as many stalls as they could, seize as much money and portable property as possible, then mount their bicycles and ride off in five different directions.

All went according to plan until the moment came for raiding the fair. On entering the temple grounds, our gangsters found a free fight already in progress! As fate would have it, the Water-Rates had planned a raid on the same temple for the very same night! Still, this was all part of the game, and the White Eagles rather enjoyed the extra excitement. But there was worse to come! The Police had got wind of what was afoot, and had concealed a body of thirty men in the village, all armed with rifles. A couple of shots fired into the air struck terror into the hearts of the struggling gangsters.

At the moment when the Police appeared on the scene, Boon Mee was engaged in a scuffle with no less a personage than Duang Keow, the leader of the Water-Rats. As Duang Keow was about twice his size, our hero decided to run for it, but before turning to flee he managed somehow to land a fairly hard blow on the Water-Rat's nose. This was more than Duang Keow could brook. Before Boon Mee could break clear, his opponent had planted his knife fairly and squarely between his shoulder-blades. Boon Mee stumbled into a near-by dry ditch, where he lay moaning.

At the same moment, Kampan, chased by a policeman, ran by.

"Do not take me away yet," he pleaded, after he had been arrested. "My younger brother has just fallen into that ditch, and I think he is hurt. Let me go to him."

"Shut your mouth," answered the policeman. "You cannot fool me with a yarn like that. You want to do a bolt, that's all. Come along with me."

*   *   *

The total number of White Eagles and Water-Rats engaged in the raid was ninety. Thirty escaped, and sixty were hauled away to the police station in the city. Of these, all those bearing arms of any kind were kept in the lock-up. The rest, numbering only ten, were allowed out on bail, after depositing their watches, bicycles, and any money they had with them, as security.

Kampan, who, as soon as he caught sight of the police, had taken the precaution of throwing away his knife, was among those released. Sorrowfully he made his way home

"What has happened?" asked his mother. "Where have you been? Where is my Little One?"

"Mother, Mother, I have been a fool and a scoundrel. I have been out with the White Eagles, and Boon Mee persuaded me to take him with me. We had a fight with the Water-Rats. The police intervened, and caught most of us, but they let me out on bail because I had no weapon."

"But where is my Little One? What have you done with him?"

"I saw him struggling with one of the Water-Rats, and he fell into a dry ditch."

"He is hurt! He is wounded! I know it! Take me to him at once. Your uncle, Noi Lah, has a bicycle taxi. Go and get it at once, and take me to Samrit village. Do not waste a moment."

In a few minutes they were on their way to Samrit, Kampan pedalling for all he was worth. It did not take him long to cover the five miles.

"Take me to the ditch where you saw my Little One fall."

At last they came to the dry ditch. There, just visible in the dark, lay a garish figure; gaudy shirt, tight black trousers, dark goggles. But still, perfectly still.

The agonised woman clambered down into the ditch and knelt beside her son.

"My Little One, my Little One, speak to me. What have they done to you?"

But her Little One lay quite still, and made no reply.

*   *   *

EXCELLENT MERIT

"Reverend Father," said Lung Wan, "I have come to ask your advice. You are a very old and a very holy man, and I know you will give me good counsel. I have spent the past four years visiting all the most sacred temples and shrines in the Kingdom, and have exhausted a great part of my savings in merit-making, in the hope that at last a son might be born to my wife and myself; but it has all been in vain. What more can I do?"

Lung Wan was an elderly Thai farmer, living in a small village near the city of Chiengmai, in Northern Thailand. He was not poor; he owned a good house, a broad and fertile rice-field, several buffaloes, and had a little money in the savings bank. He was now fifty years of age, and had been married for thirty years. He and his wife, Nang Som, had but one sorrow. They had no children. The longing for a child, preferably a boy, had become an obsession with them both. Now, after consulting holy men throughout the realm, and praying in dozens of temples, Lung Wan at last bethought himself of seeking the advice of Phramaha Prasert, the abbot of the monastery in his own native village.

"My son," answered the venerable abbot, "I know no more about such matters than you do. But it seems to me that perhaps you have been mistaken in wandering so far afield in search of a remedy for your trouble. This monastery, here in your own village, is the place where you and your parents, and all your ancestors for generations back, have been making merit, feeding the monks, helping to repair the buildings, and performing other worthy acts. Your father, I remember when I was a young man, was actually a monk here for two years, and you yourself served as a novice when you were a boy. You have accumulated more merit here than anywhere else, but you have never prayed for a son in your own temple, nor laid your troubles at the feet of our own great golden image of the Lord Buddha. Why not come tomorrow, with your wife, bringing a few offerings for the temple, and here, close to your own home, pray for the blessing you so earnestly desire? I, too, will add my prayers to yours."

"Reverend Father!" exclaimed Lung Wan. "I am sure you are right. Why did I never think of this before?"

So on the very next day, along came Lung Wan and Nang Som, bringing with them food for the four monks and five novices in the monastery, and quantities of candles and incense sticks to light in the temple. Then they knelt together before the great image, and prayed with a fervour they had never

72

felt before. For more than an hour they knelt there praying; then they arose, and Lung Wan said to Nang Som:— "Wife, I feel peace and hope in my heart. The Holy One smiled at me!"

Many of the Thai sculptors of olden days possessed great skill. They often succeeded in representing the Lord Buddha with a gentle smile on His face — a smile of peace and sympathy. Lung Wan had seen the great image hundreds of times before, but he had never noticed that gentle smile. Now he noticed it, and fancied it was meant for him. Maybe it was.

Less than a year later, the prayers of Lung Wan and Nang Som were answered. Nang Som gave birth to a baby boy. He was the most beautiful baby that had been seen in the village within living memory, perfect feature, strong, healthy limbs, skin like burnished bronze. But, alas! He had one defect. This little child, perfect in every other respect, had a club-foot. His left foot was twisted and distorted, terrible to behold.

However, Lung Wan and his wife did not worry themselves unduly about the club-foot. They had a son, a beautiful, strong, healthy son. What did a little blemish like a club-foot matter to them?

The little boy was named by his parents Boon Sri, or Excellent Merit.

A month after the birth of Boon Sri, his father and mother carried him to the temple, and laid him at the feet of the great image.

"It is through the merit accumulated in this temple," said Lung Wan, "that this child was born to us. Therefore I have named him Excellent Merit, and I promise that as soon as he is old enough, he shall be ordained as a novice here, and now-here else."

The years passed by, and Boon Sri grew to be a very strong, sturdy boy. Though he walked with a limp, he managed to play badminton and basket-ball with the other boys at the village school. Moreover, he was quick to learn, and always held a high place in his class.

Until he was ten years of age, his club-foot never worried him at all. It was just a defect which was there, which had

73

always been there, and which could not be helped. Then something happened which changed the boy's life, and cast a shadow over his whole existence.

A local newspaper published a series of photographs of schoolboys and schoolgirls who had passed highest in that year's Government examinations. Boon Sri had passed first among the entrants from Standard III, and his picture was published in the paper. One of his schoolfellows, Ai Peng, who had passed second, and who was a spiteful and malicious boy, said to him:— "You may be all right in an examination, but you will never be of any use in the world with that ugly, deformed foot. Moreover, your father is planning to commit a great sin. He brags all over the place that he intends to have you ordained as a novice next year. Maybe he thinks that he will acquire "excellent merit" by having you invested with the yellow robe, but *my* father says that a novice ought to be physically perfect, not a boy with a blind eye, or a hare-lip, or a club-foot. To ordain monstrosities of that kind, *my* father says, is certain to bring misfortune to the monastery and to the Lord Abbot."

Boon Sri's heart stood still. He turned and went away without saying a word. But from that moment he knew no more happiness. He worked and played as before, but he was tormented day and night by the thought that he was deformed and hideous, and by the fear that once his distorted body was invested with the yellow robe, some terrible misfortune would befall the monastery or the old abbot, whom he had always looked upon as a second father.

He could not bring himself to say anything to his parents about this, knowing that their hearts were set upon his ordination taking place, but at last, when he was nearly eleven years old, and the time for his entry into the monastery was drawing near, he went secretly to lay his troubles before the abbot.

"My son," said the old man, "what Ai Peng said to you was cruel and wicked. Moreover, it was false. It is true that a blind boy cannot become a novice, but that is only because he would be unable to perform his duties. Your twisted foot will not hamper you to any extent. If your heart is pure, if you try to fulfil the vows you will be called upon

74

to take, if you forget yourself, and think only of others, you will bring nothing but blessings to the monastery and to me. Only cruelty, dishonesty, falsehood, impurity and insobriety can bring ill luck to the monastery. Keep free from such sins as these, and you need fear nothing."

Boon Sri was a little happier when he heard these words; but he could not quite forget what Ai Peng had said. Every morning and every night he prayed that his club-foot might be cured, and that he might become like other boys

At last the great day dawned, the day which was to see Boon Sri bid farewell to the world and join the community of Buddhist monks and novices. Spiteful Ai Peng, too, was to be ordained on the same day.

After breakfast, which was to be their only solid meal that day, the two boys were taken to the house of the village headman. There they were dressed in the gorgeous garments and glittering ornaments of ancient kings, golden crowns were set on their heads, and brocaded, gem-encrusted shoes were put on their feet. Their faces were thickly powdered, their cheeks artistically rouged, their lips carmined. Everybody said they looked like little angels. They were then mounted on two gaily decorated white ponies, and set out for the monastery. Accompanying them were hundreds of their friends and neighbours, young and old, men and women, boys and girls, singing and cheering, beating drums, playing on trumpets and flutes. For when a man or boy is bidding farewell to the pomps and glories of the world to don the yellow robe of a Buddhist monk, it is only fitting that the world he is leaving should be, for the moment, as full of pomp and glory as possible.

I sometimes think that a little Thai boy, riding at the head of a procession on the day of his ordination, clad in spangled garments, with a crown on his head, is the proudest and happiest creature in the whole world. To Ai Peng this was a glorious and wonderful day; but Boon Sri felt no elation; he could not forget what Ai Peng had said to him:— "You will bring ill luck to the monastery and to the Lord Abbot." He looked down at his left foot, hidden by a gilded shoe, and encrusted with gems, and thought to himself:— "All this is a sham. I am a miserable, deformed creature, with a hideous club-foot, unworthy to wear the yellow robe of a novice."

At last the procession reached the temple. The two boys dismounted, and were led to the monks' quarters. There they were divested of their glittering garments and their golden crowns. After that, their heads and eye-brows were shaved with a brass razor, and they were taken to bathe at the well. then they were dressed in white robes and conducted to the temple building. All the neighbours who had taken part in the procession, and many other people, knelt on the floor of the temple, with the two white-robed boys in front of them. The abbot, seated cross-legged on a raised dais, preached a short sermon, expounding the duties of a novice. Then he called upon the boys to take the five essential vows:—

I will kill no sentient being.
I will steal no man's property.
I will speak no falsehood.
I will keep my body in chastity.
I will drink no intoxicating liquor.

After this, they were required to take five supplementary vows, binding only on monks and novices. These are:—

I will eat no food after midday.
I will not dance or listen to music.
I will not deck myself with flowers or use perfume.
I will not sleep on a high bedstead.
I will not touch gold or silver.

Then all the monks and novices, nine in number, chanted a psalm. The two boys took off their white robes, and were invested with the yellow robes of Buddhist novices. The congregation dispersed, leaving Boon Sri and Ai Peng, now full-fledged novices, kneeling in the temple.

Night came on. The two boys, tired out after a strenuous day, were taken to sleep on the verandah of the monks' quarters. But Boon Sri could not sleep. He had been called upon to do a good deal of praying that day, but there was one more prayer in his heart, still unexpressed in words, which he felt he must utter before dawn.

A little before midnight, he crept silently across to the temple, bearing with him seven wax candles and seven sticks

76

of incense. He lighted these, and then knelt down before the great image of the Lord Buddha. There, on the very spot where, twelve years before, his parents had prayed that a son might be given to them, he knelt and prayed.

"Holy One," he whispered, "I have not come here to pray that my club-foot may be cured. I have borne with it for eleven years, and I promise to make the best of it from now on, without ever complaining. But grant only that I may not be the cause of any ill luck to this temple and monastery, where my parents and ancestors have worshipped and made merit for so many years, or to the good old Lord Abbot, who has always been my best friend."

As he uttered these words, he looked up at the face of the great image. He saw the kindly smile on the Holy One's lips, and he fancied, as his father had done years before, that the smile was intended for him. Then he thought that he heard a soft, gentle voice, saying:— "Do not be unhappy, little boy, everything will be all right."

Boon Sri stood up. In that same instant, he knew that a marvellous change had come over him. He felt that he was standing up straight, not lobsidedly as he had stood all his life. He turned, and walked to the door of the temple. His first few steps were faltering and uncertain; then he became accustomed to the new sensation, and walked boldly and firmly to the temple door.

The old abbot had been sleeping badly. A little after midnight he arose and went to lean over his verandah for a breath of fresh air. Then he noticed a faint gleam of light coming from the temple. Wondering who could be there at that late hour, he came down from his house and went across to investigate. When he came near the temple, he saw little Boon Sri standing all alone in the doorway. He felt at once that there was something strange and unusual about the boy's appearance. Then he realised that Boon Sri was standing perfectly upright.

"Come down the steps, my son," he called out.

Boon Sri came slowly down, walking firmly and uprightly, with no trace of a limp. He approached the old man, and knelt at his feet.

"Reverend Father," he said, "I remembered your advice to try to forget myself and to think of others. I told the Holy One that my club-foot did not matter, and begged Him to let no ill luck befall this monastery, where my family have worshipped for so many years, or to you, whom I love so dearly. And the Holy One smiled at me, and whispered to me, saying that everything would be all right. In that same moment, my club-foot was cured, and became just like the foot of any other boy. Look at it and see!"

The old man bent down, and looked in wonder at the boy's foot. Then he said:— "Your parents named you Excellent Merit, and surely you have gained excellent merit this night, by forgetting your own troubles, and thinking only of this temple and monastery, and of me, your old friend and teacher. But I must be sure, absolutely sure. I know some would think it unseemly for a novice to run about in the temple grounds at night. But I must be sure. Run as fast as you can to yonder pagoda and back again!"

Hitching up his yellow robe, Boon Sri ran across to the pagoda. It was a marvellous sight to see this little boy, who less than an hour before had been a cripple, running in the bright moonlight, running swiftly and surely, beautiful and graceful as a young fawn. When he reached the pagoda, he stood there for a few moments with his arms outstretched, as though he wanted to embrace the old abbot, and the monastery, and the whole world beyond; then he ran swiftly back, and knelt again at the abbot's feet.

"Tomorrow at dawn," said the old man, "we will go to tell your parents of the wonderful thing which has come to pass. By noon, the whole city will know of it. The Chiengmai Radio Station will broadcast the news to the whole Kingdom. In the evening, the Bangkok Station will make it known to the entire world. Newspaper-men, photographers and sightseers will throng this temple and monastery. You may even be taken to see the King and Queen. Makers of cinema films will offer you vast sums to go to foreign countries and act for them. A thousand temptations will assail you. What will you do?"

And the little boy replied:— "I will stay here with you, Holy Father, and do my duty in this monastery, where such a wonderful blessing has been granted to me. I will stay here until I am a man. After that, who can tell?"

"My son," said the abbot, "I knew that you would answer me as you have done. But come with me now; we will go up into the temple, and kneel in thankfulness before the image of the Holy One. Tomorrow our secret will be the property of the whole world. Tonight it belongs to us alone; to you and me."

So the old man and the little boy went up together into the temple, where Boon Sri's seven candles and incense sticks were still smouldering, and knelt side by side before the image of the Lord Buddha. And the great golden image looked down upon them and smiled.

WAS I RIGHT?

It is great sin to swear unto a sin,
But greater sin to keep a sinful oath.
Who can be bound by any solemn vow
To do a murderous deed, to rob a man,
To force a spotless virgin's chastity,
And have no other reason for this wrong
But that he was bound by a solemn oath?

Shakespeare, King Henry the Sixth.

Casually picking up my volume of Shakespeare's plays the other day, I came across these lines. They recalled to my memory the occasion, a few years ago, when I was faced by this exact problem — whether to break my word or to keep my promise to do something which I felt to be wrong. This is how it happened:—

I had borrowed a Jeep from my friend, Nai Sawang Chompu, and was on my way to Ban Me Dua, about sixty miles North of Chiengmai, to take a few photographs of the Borneo Company's elephants dragging teak logs. We had met with a series of delays and mishaps, and it was already dark

79

when we reached the village of Me Larp, which is about half-way between Chiengmai and Ban Me Dua. As we left the village, a tall young man, wearing the uniform of a Police Corporal, held up his hand. He was a smart-looking fellow, had a small black moustache, was wearing black goggles, and spoke in a very gruff bass voice. We stopped, and the young man very politely asked the driver if he could give him a lift to another village, a few miles along the road. The driver agreed. I was sitting on the front seat with the driver. The young man got up behind, and off we went.

We had not gone for more than about ten miles when I was touched from behind on the shoulder. Turning round, I saw that our passenger was pointing a revolver at the back of the driver's head.

"There is a forest road to the left a short way ahead," said he. "Tell the driver to go along it for about a hundred metres and then stop. Otherwise......."

The driver did not need any telling. He turned off along the forest road, drove for a hundred metres or so, and stopped. In stopping, however, he deliberately drove the Jeep against a tree. The shock of the impact made me and our passenger fall forward, and in the confusion the driver jumped down from the Jeep and vanished into the forest.

"Let him go," said our passenger. "I don't want him. You are the man with the money. Hand it over quick, before the driver can reach the next village and give the alarm."

"How much money do you think I have?" I asked. "I have only seventy-five bahts on me."

"Nonsense," answered he, "you are the Nai Hang Borneo, taking out enormous sums of money to pay your forest staff's wages. Hand over quick, or I will shoot you dead."

"Look at me well," said I. "I am a very old man. Have you ever seen a man of my age running a teak forest? I am only going to the forest to take pictures of the elephants working."

He took a good look at me. His face fell. "What!" he exclaimed. "I have taken all this trouble to get a miserable seventy-five bahts! Anyhow, hand it over!"

By this time I was beginning to size up the desperado a bit. He seemed to grow younger and younger, his voice had become less and less gruff, and as I looked carefully at him, it dawned upon me that his moustache was a fake — drawn on his upper lip with a bit of charcoal!

"Look here," I said to him, "you are a very young chap. Why do you want to hold up a car in this way? You will surely be tracked down and arrested, and your whole life will be ruined."

"But I am going to shoot you dead," said he, "and there will be nobody to identify me. The driver hardly looked at me at all. All he thought about was to make himself scarce as quickly as possible."

"I can see that you are really a very nice boy," said I. "Surely you would not murder an old man like me. Clear out, and we'll forget all about it."

"No!" said he. "The driver will give information. I may be arrested, and you will be asked to identify me. I am sorry, but I shall have to shoot you unless you solemnly promise me not to do so."

"But can you trust me to keep my word?" I asked.

"You are an Englishman," he replied. "I have been told that an Englishman always keeps his word."

This was altogether too much for me. "All right, all right," said I. "I will give you my word. What is more, I will give you forty bahts for a present. Now clear out quickly, while you have time." As I said this, the whimsical aspect of the situation caught my fancy, and I burst out laughing. The dangerous robber joined in.

"Thanks very much, Sir," said he, shaking with mirth. "You are just the sort of man I like. Goodnight. And, remember, you promised me!"

So saying, he leapt down from the Jeep and vanished into the forest.

As soon as I had managed to re-start the Jeep, the driver, who had been hiding all the time in the forest close by, came back. I did not tell him all that had passed, only that the robber, finding that he had mistaken our Jeep for one belonging to the Borneo Company, and disappointed in his expectation of making a big haul, had cleared off. So on we went to Ban Me Dua. Next day, I took my elephant photographs, and we drove back to Chiengmai. We stopped on the way at Me Larp, where the driver reported the attempt which had been made to rob us to the local Police.

About a week later, I received a letter from the Chief of Police at Chiengmai, asking me to go the next day to Ban Me Dua to identify a man who had been arrested there on suspicion of being the robber who had held up Nai Sawang's Jeep.

Next morning I drove to Ban Me Dua, and proceeded to the Police Station. The first person I saw was my friend the desperado. He looked younger, smaller, and altogether more harmless than he had looked when wearing black goggles and a phony moustache. He had handcuffs on his wrists, and looked the picture of misery.

"Is this the man?" asked the Officer in charge.

I looked at the young prisoner, and his eyes seemed almost to shout at me:— "You promised, you promised! An Englishman always keeps his word. You promised!"

"Now," thought I to myself, "the fatal moment has come. To lie, or not to lie. If I speak the truth, I shall be breaking my word, and sending a foolish young lad to jail — maybe ruining his whole life. If I lie, I shall be deceiving the Police and obstructing the course of justice. There is no half-way course. If I say I am not sure, they will probably press on with the case, and I shall have to go through with it all over again in Court, where I shall be on oath. Now, or never! Here goes!"

I took a deep breath, swallowed, and said firmly and boldly:— "This is *not* the man. The robber I met that night was older and tougher. Moreover, he had a moustache."

"Well, then," said the Police Officer. "That settles it. We relied entirely on your evidence. The driver barely saw the man, but he, too, described him as having a moustache. We have nothing else to go on but suspicion. This young man is the brother of a Police Corporal, and so had access to a police uniform and a revolver. But we shall have to let him go."

Was I right, or was I wrong? I have never been able to make up my mind about this. But, anyhow, my story has a sequel. Here it is:—

About two years after I had committed, as Shakespeare says, "the greater sin, to keep a sinful oath," I was sitting one morning in my study, when in walked a stalwart and good-looking young man. At first I did not recognise him as the "criminal" whom I had last seen at Ban Me Dua, wearing handcuffs, and looking thoroughly deflated. He was very smartly dressed, and bore himself with all the *panache* of the young Police Corporal who had threatened to shoot me dead. In his hand he bore a carved teak elephant. When I realised who my visitor was, I experienced a real delight to see him looking so self-assured and so prosperous.

"Sir," said he, "I have come to thank you for keeping your promise to me, and saving me from going to jail, which would have ruined me for life. I am now doing very well. I have a shop where I make and sell carved elephants, and I have brought you one of them for a present."

"Thank you for the beautiful elephant," I replied; "but I hardly think I ought to accept it. It is a reward for having committed a great sin, making a false statement to the Police, which has tormented my conscience ever since. Still, I am glad to know that the evil-doer I helped to turn loose on society is not so vile a criminal as he appeared to be."

He seized me by the hand, and with tears in his eyes, said:— "Do not think of me as a criminal. I was only sixteen years old when I tried to carry out that foolish robbery. It was all done on the spur of the moment. I had lost all my money gambling, and when I heard that the Borneo Company were sending up a Jeep with a vast sum of money to Ban Me Dua, I yielded to a sudden temptation. My elder brother is a Police Corporal. I borrowed his uniform, took an old revolver which was lying about in the house, and — well, you know the rest! Please do not think that I really intended to shoot you dead. That would have been impossible The revolver was useless. The cylinder would not turn and the trigger would not work. And, anyhow, I had no cartridges! My firearm was as phony as my moustache!"

And so we parted, laughing as heartily as we had done

in the forest two years before. I somehow felt that he was just the sort of robber I liked.

But I am still not sure whether I acted rightly or not.

* * *

THE MAN WHO COULD NOT BE ALONE

"Are you a woman, Noi Insom," asked Groves, "or are you a child, that you fear to go alone round a turn or two of the stream?"

His frank young Saxon face bore an expression of contempt as he looked at the sturdy young Thai beside him. A strange contrast they formed, standing there, side by side in the bed of the Huey Me Si Pan stream, that difficult thoroughfare which many travellers in Northern Siam know all too well; he who would pass from the town of Nan to the north must trudge for seven miles through those waters; to the right and left are lofty precipices surmounted by endless tracts of impenetrable jungle, and down in the deep valley of the stream, over its slippery rocks and through its deep blue pools lies the only direct highway. When the rains swell these waters, the wayfarer pitches his tent and waits at the head or the foot of the valley for a day — a week — a month, until the torrent subsides, and smiles as he thinks of the far-off lands where time is money and not merely an unimportant fragment of eternity.

Groves stamped his foot impatiently, and again addressed his servant:—

"Must *I* then go back for the stick, coward? When we get back to Nan, I will buy a skirt for you to wear!"

"Do not be angry, Nai. I am not afraid of any *man*. Have I not my gun with me, and do you not know that I can hold my own in the boxing ring with any fighter in Nan. Did you not see me fight Ai Pong, the champion of Lampang, on the King's birthday three weeks ago, and knock him out in two rounds? It is not a *man* whom I fear. But here comes

Ai Keo; he and I will go back together and bring your stick from the place where you left it."

Groves sat down and waited for the two young men to return, wondering what strange new form of superstition he had run his head against. Noi Insom had been but three months in his service. He was an active, and, apparently, plucky youth, but he showed a most strange reluctance to be left alone in the house, and since the present journey had been undertaken, he had displayed a positive terror at the thought of walking by himself in the jungle. Since they had entered the Me Si Pan stream some two hours before, at daybreak, he had stuck to his master like a leech, and when he was asked to return to recover the stick, dropped but a few minutes before, he had politely, but firmly, refused to comply.

Groves' ill-humour was quickly over. When Noi Insom and Ai Keo returned with the stick a few minutes later, he merely laughed at the former's apologetic expression, then rose and continued on his way. Noi Insom, as before, kept close behind him.

"Why do you follow me so close, Noi Insom? Why are you so different from the rest of my men, who always lag behind? What is it that you fear? Tell me! I will not laugh at you."

"Nai, you are a foreigner, and I have been told that in foreign lands there are no evil spirits, such as are met with in this country. I also know that foreigners do not trouble themselves about such matters, and that some of them have never even heard of the fierce things which surround us. Tell me, Nai," — and his voice was lowered to a whisper — "have you ever heard of the Phi-Bawp?"

Groves had heard the name, and understood vaguely that it signified some kind of legendary being of the vampire tribe. But his information on the subject was scanty, and he craved for more.

"Nai, I will tell you about the Phi-Bawp, and I will tell you also why I, Noi Insom, fear them more than other men do; for indeed it is on account of them that I never remain

85

alone. And in truth, I fear to be alone in this Me Si Pan stream more than in any other place."

*   *   *

"You must know," he continued, "that any person may be a Phi-Bawp, and it is rare for people to know who is or is not one. Some are men and some are women. Some have become Phi-Bawps owing to their own evil nature, and some in spite of themselves. In the daytime they go about their business like other folk, but at night they creep out to perform their wicked works. If they see a sick man, they enter into his body by night, and they eat away his life, and drink the blood of his heart. And when they can find no victims, then they satisfy their hateful appetites with even more dreadful meals. Often none of their friends know of the evil spirit which possesses them, for the Phi-Bawp have two bodies. Thus a husband may see his wife lying in peaceful sleep beside him, yet at that same moment she is in some distant place, doing horrible deeds of cruelty or loathsomeness. I have even heard of young infants who were Phi-Bawp, and who, while seemingly asleep in their mothers' arms, were wandering about seeking the lives of their neighbours or doing hateful works in the graveyard."

"A year ago I was a Corporal in the Police at Nan; you have often remarked on my erect walk, and wondered at my replying smartly when you spoke to me. That was from the drill."

"One day the Captain took me and six other men on duty to Muang Suat, the village which we will reach in a couple of hours. We camped the first night on the very camping-ground where you camped last night, but owing to many delays it was late in the second afternoon before we reached Muang Suat. Hardly had we arrived there when the Captain discovered that he had by mischance left behind a small revolver, even as you left your stick by the stream just now. At once I volunteered to go back for it, and my friend Ai Puan offered to go with me."

"We set out just before dusk, and we hoped by walking quickly to reach the camping-ground in four hours or so. There we would sleep the night, returning early the next morning. We had some fear of wild beasts, but we were both armed with rifles, and both of us knew the way very well."

"The moon rose early that night, but you will understand, Nai, that in this Me Si Pan stream one sees but little moonlight, for the high rocks and thick forest hide the moon's face. Nevertheless, there were streaks of light along the way; so by looking ahead to the places where the light was shining, and trusting to the glow of our lanterns in the darker passages, we did not find the way very difficult."

"At first we sang as we went along as most Thai travellers are wont to do at night, but as we approached the head-waters of the stream we were getting a little breathless, so we walked on in silence."

"Suddenly our lantern spluttered and went out. Ai Puan took a box of matches from his pocket, but before he had lit a match, the box slipped from his fingers and fell into the stream. I had two boxes, but they were in the knapsack on my back. I lifted the strap over my head, and began to grope in the sack for the matches. While I was doing this, Ai Puan gripped me sharply by the arm. I looked up."

"We were in a place where the stream stretched straight along ahead of us. There was no bend. The banks were high and rocky, and scarcely a single ray of the moon was visible; yet as I looked I saw, coming slowly towards us, two pale green lights. Not smoothly did they come, but rising and sinking, in the same manner as the head of a man walking over a surface covered with rocks and boulders."

"I had often been told that the Phi-Bawp give forth by night a pale green glimmer, but I had never heard any tale of their being seen far away from the town in the distant forest. Nevertheless, the thought of them came instantly to my mind when I saw these lights. Ai Puan told me afterwards that his thought was the same as mine. But at the time we neither of us spoke. Something within us seemed to warn us that our only hope of safety lay in remaining silent and concealing ourselves. We were not in the centre of the valley, but near a large boulder at the side, so that we had no difficulty in squatting down together without making any noise, concealing ourselves partly by means of the boulder, and partly by pressing our backs against the ferns which grew thickly on the steep bank."

"Ai Puan held my right hand in his left, and thus we waited for the green lights to pass by."

"Nai, these lights were very dim. They did not light up the sides of the stream at all, but we could see their reflection faintly in the water as they came nearer. Not until they were quite close to us did I see that they were human faces, and that beneath them were the shadowy forms of bodies."

"Nearer still they came, walking just as an ordinary man might walk, and then I saw that they were carrying between them some dark object. Yet a few steps more, and by the light of their faces I beheld that it was the dead body of a child. I felt no wonder at the sight. It was not until later that I asked myself whence they came that night, or why they were bearing their pitiful burden through the Me Si Pan stream so late. At the time my only thought was the hope that they might pass by without seeing us."

"On they came, nearer and nearer, until they were hidden from our view by the boulder behind which we were crouching. Then Ai Puan trembled. I felt his hand shake as it held mine, and in the same moment a little stone was dislodged from the bank behind his back, and fell, with a sharp clatter, onto the rocks at our feet."

"My heart stood still, and cold drops of sweat oozed from the skin of my forehead. Then a thing happened which made me feel as though I were already dead and cold; two luminous green faces appeared above the top of the boulder and gazed at us as we crouched there trembling amidst the ferns. Dim and pale was the light of those two faces. I remember now that, even in my terror, I noticed the beams of that light shining with a feeble reflection on the nickel buttons of Ai Puan's coat."

"Nai, the glimmering features of those two faces were features which I knew well! Even now, I dare not tell you the names of those two men who looked at me over that rock, but this I will say — that you know them both! Within this past week you have spoken to both of them, and they are well known to all who dwell at Nan. No doubt that night they

88

were seemingly lying in harmless slumber, yet Ai Puan and I crouched at the side of the Me Si Pan stream and looked into their eyes across a rocky boulder."

"One thing I cannot understand, and that is why they did not slay us then, when they knew we had watched them bearing their little victim. Some say that the Phi-Bawp never seek to kill two who are together, fearing that one may escape them. However that may be, we suffered no harm that night. The green faces were slowly withdrawn, and a few moments later we saw them go falteringly on their way along the stream, and by the faint light around them, we could still see the dark form which they were bearing between them."

"Not until they were out of sight did we dare to move. Then we arose and started to run like men stricken with madness. Onwards we ran, sometimes falling over stones, sometimes tearing our clothes on the undergrowth, only seeking to reach the camping-round, and both hoping, with a frantic hope, that we should find some other travellers encamped there."

"How long we took I cannot say, but at last we flung ourselves exhausted on the ground in the midst of a party of Shan traders who were spending the night in the very spot, Nai, where you slept last night. Great was their surprise when two policemen rushed so madly into their midst, torn and dishevelled, covered with mud, scratched and bleeding, trembling with fear."

" 'These fellows are drunk,' they said."

*   *   *

"The next morning we found the Captain's revolver, but we dared not return with it to Muang Suat. Indeed, so great was our fear that we decided, after consulting together, that there was nothing else for us to do but to desert from the Police Force and escape away to some other part of the country. We therefore concealed our uniforms and rifles in the forest, together with the Captain's revolver, and set out for Nan, intending to bid farewell to our relations there before going away."

"But a great misfortune befell us almost immediately. We had only gone a short way when we met a party of Police under the command of a Lieutenant. Knowing that we were

89

supposed to be on duty at Maung Suat, and finding us returning to Nan wearing nothing but our underclothes, the Lieutenant had us arrested."

"When the Captain returned to Nan, we were charged with desertion and with stealing the Captain's revolver. We showed the place where we had hidden it, together with our uniforms and rifles, but nobody would believe that our intentions were innocent, since we could give no reason for wishing to desert. So great was our fear of the Phi-Bawp that we did not dare to utter a word concerning our experiences in the Me Si Pan stream; and without a doubt, had we done so, it would have seemed but an empty lie invented to excuse ourselves. In the end, the Court sentenced us each to six months' imprisonment. So, with chains on our legs, we worked hard day by day, carting stones along the road, and doing other heavy labour. Murderers and thieves were our companions, and hard boards our nightly resting-place."

"While we were in the jail we often took counsel together as to how we might best escape the vengeance of the Phi-Bawp, calling to our minds all the stories we had heard concerning them. We hoped that, as we had suffered ourselves to be cast into prison rather than divulge what we had seen, we might perhaps be spared, yet nevertheless we decided that it would above all things be most unwise for either of us ever to go out alone either by day or by night."

"But soon something happened which showed me all too clearly that our fears were justified, and our hopes of escape but vain."

"Ai Puan disappeared! How or when he went nobody seemed exactly to know. He was sent with a gang of eight other men and two warders to take a cartload of timber along the road to the old city. On the way back he was missed. Whether he loitered behind, or how it happened, nobody appeared to know for certain, but it was assumed that he had escaped. I, of course, knew better; but I said nothing. I kept my mouth shut then, and for all the rest of the time that I remained in the jail. And indeed, Nai, except for my old mother and yourself, nobody has ever heard my story."

"So now, Nai, you will understand the reason why I never go about alone. Whether it be light or dark, I never allow myself to remain even for a moment in a place where I have no other person in sight. Perhaps you may doubt me, and think that I have invented this tale to hide the fact that I am in truth a thief. But ask yourself first this question. How can a man keep on for ever feigning a fear which he does not really feel?"

*   *   *

Groves said nothing, but lit his pipe and walked steadily forward, closely followed by Noi Insom.

His commonsense assured him that the whole tale was an ingenious romance intended to attach a mysterious interest to Noi Insom's unfortunate experience of "six months hard," which the latter must know could not long be kept a secret The mere fact of the said "six months" left him unmoved, for he had been long enough in Siam to have acquired a philosophical view of such little mishaps, which, indeed, many excellent people look upon in much the same light as an attack of measles or chicken-pox.

Nevertheless, Groves had been in some measure impressed by his servant's earnestness; while the man's unwillingness to be left alone stood forth as an undeniable fast, whatever the cause thereof might be. Reason, of course, could guide to but one conclusion, but most of those who have lived long enough in Siam know very well that there are some matters in regard to which commonsense is not a faultless guide.

But other and more important matters had soon to be considered, and by the next morning, when Groves, after camping for the night at Muang Suat, set forth with all his party, on their northward march, all thought of Noi Insom and the Phi-Bawp had for the time being passed from his mind.

*   *   *

A month passed by. Once again Groves was splashing along through the same Me Si Pan stream, but this time Southwards on his homeward journey to Nan

Alone he trudged, for none of the shorter brown legs among his party could keep up with his long strides. The faithful Noi Insom, who usually clung to him like a limpet, had cut his foot the day before on a sharp stone, so had perforce to content himself with the company of Maung Shwe Bya, the Burmese clerk, a portly gentleman, who usually made his journeys on the back of an equally portly pony, but was today waddling along as best he could over the slippery stones of the stream; for one needs a steady seat and a hard heart to ride a pony in the Me Si Pan stream.

So Groves trudged on until midday brought thoughts of lunch. Then he seated himself on a rock in the stream and waited for the arrival of the tardy carrier, whose advent always seemed slow in direct proportion to the keenness of his master's appetite.

Five minutes later, fat Maung Shwe Bya appeared round the bend of the stream, alone. He seated himself on another rock, mopped his brow and anathematized in voluble Burmese the stones, the water, and the blister on his left foot.

"Where is Noi Insom?" asked Groves.

"Ah Sir, as for Noi Insom, I cannot wait for him. His foot it swell so he cannot keep with me. He beg and beg me to wait for him, but I have enough trouble already with my blister, and I will not make more brother waiting for Noi Insom. He go too slow. So I tell him to wait for Ai La who come behind with Your Honour's tiffin."

Five minutes more, and Ai La rounded the corner with the tiffin basket.

"Where is Noi Insom?" again asked Groves.

"I have not seen him since we started this morning. He has been ahead of me all the way."

"But he stayed behind only a few minutes ago to wait for you, so Maung Shwee Bya tells me."

"I have not seen him."

Suddenly a feeling of fear took possession of Groves' mind. True, it was absurd to suppose that any harm could have come to the man in the few minutes that had elapsed since Maung Shwe Bya left him. It was midday. The sun was shining.

Nevertheless, Groves could not forget the abject fear which Noi Insom had always shown at the thought of being left alone, even for a moment; he thought of the strange tale he had heard about that uncanny midnight encounter in the

Me Si Pan stream, possibly only a few yards from the spot where he now stood; he remembered the disappearance of Ai Puan; in spite of the noonday heat he shivered slightly: for an uneasiness, of which he was half ashamed had overcome him.

"Come," he said, "let us all go back and find out why Noi Insom is loitering so much today."

The three of them turned and walked back along the stream. Only two or three minutes later, Maung Shwe Bya stopped.

"Here is where I left him, Sir, seated on that stone." He pointed to a large rock a yard or so away from the bed of the stream, but partly surrounded by a pool left by the last rise of the variable waters.

Then, as he looked more closely, he started. His voice was shrill with fear.

"Sir!" he almost shrieked, "the pool! Look at the pool!"

Groves looked. The water of the pool was red.

When the rest of the party came up, every man searched for many hours. They examined every inch of the stream. The scanned the almost inaccessible banks for footprints.

It was useless. Noi Insom had vanished, leaving no trace behind, save only the red stain in the waters of the pool.

*　　　*　　　*

THE WATCH

On New Year's Day the Old Nai gave his young servant Somboon a beautiful Swiss wristlet watch. It was chromium-plated, antimagnetic, waterproof, dustproof and stainless; moreover, it contained seventeen jewels. Somboon had never before owned so delectable an article; he liked it better even than his Raleigh sports bicycle, which he had saved up for over a year to buy.

For a week Somboon spent half his time looking at his watch, comparing it with the clocks in the hall and the sitting-room, and checking it with the chimes of Big Ben, heard from afar on the Old Nai's radio. He decided that it kept better time than any of them.

Then came tragedy. Somboon had taken his Old Nai's little dog Whisky to wash at the river landing. He took off his shirt and shorts and laid them on the landing, with the new watch on top. Then he went down the steps and carefully soaped Whisky all over; but when he was about to dip him in the water, the little dog broke loose, ran up the steps and went to shake himself on top of Somboon's clothes — and the precious watch. Somboon ran to seize him, but the naughty little dog gave one final shake, and in so doing kicked the watch into the river. The water was over seven feet deep, with thick mud at the bottom, and there was no possible hope of retrieving the watch. Sorrowfully Somboon finished washing the dog, and then went back to the house to tell the Old Nai of his loss.

The Old Nai was not angry or annoyed. Somboon had noticed that for some time past he had given up blaming anybody for anything, however foolish or careless. All he said was:— "Do not worry, Somboon. In a short while I shall be going on a journey, and, before leaving, I will give you my gold watch."

"When are you leaving, Nai," asked Somboon. "Where are you going to, and how long will you be away?"

"I am not sure when I shall be leaving," answered the Old Nai, "but I think it will be pretty soon, and I am not likely to come back."

"Do not go away, Nai," said Somboon. "I would rather you stayed here and kept your gold watch. Maybe, if I am a good boy, in a year or so you will buy me another chromium watch."

"I fear I cannot stay here much longer," said the Old Nai. "However — wait and see."

A few days later, Somboon took up his master's early morning tea at the usual time. The Old Nai seemed to be asleep. When Somboon was about to set down the tray on the bedside table, he saw there a small parcel, marked with his name. Wonderingly, he took it up, put down the tray, and went out. Then he opened the parcel, and found in it his

.... *the naughty little dog gave one final shake, and in so doing kicked the watch into the river.*

master's gold wristlet watch. There was a card on top, bearing the message:—

> To Somboon from his Old Nai.
> Do not forget me.

Somboon's heart stood still. Why did his Nai write, "Do not forget me?" Why was he lying so still? Why had he spoken of going on a long journey? What did it all mean? Tremblingly he returned to the bedroom. The Old Nai had not moved. Somboon gently touched his hand. It was cold. He touched his cheek. Cold, cold as ice!

Then Somboon knelt weeping by the bedside.

"Nai, Nai," he sobbed, "I do not want the watch. Please do not go away. Stay here with me."

But the Old Nai said nothing.

THE MOUSE AND THE SAPPHIRE

Three Shans sat cross-legged on the floor of a tiny bamboo hut. A white cloth was spread forth in their midst, upon which lay an assortment of uncut sapphires of every size and shade.

The oldest of the three was doing most of the talking. As his mouth was filled to overflowing with betel-nut and his teeth were all loose, his conversation was not over lucid, but his views appeared to be unflattering in regard to the quality of the stone which he held up between his grimy thumb and forefinger.

The old man's countenance was not one to inspire confidence, nor indeed was that of his son, a sturdy ruffian of about forty who sat facing him. Mining towns and villages all over the world are known to be centres in which are to be found many "tough cases", and the ruby and sapphire mines of Pailin can produce as picturesque an assortment of Burmese and Shan scoundrels as it would be possible to find anywhere.

These two men, Chong Soo and Sang Hla, father and son, were well known and well feared at the mines. They had the reputation of being invulnerable, a reputation which is not difficult to obtain, but which is as a rule only useful to men whose ways are such as to render them liable to sudden attack.

The third man, Ai Seng, was a mere boy, a "tenderfoot" as he would have been called in the West. He, like many others, had left his country and settled at Pailin in the hope of making a speedy fortune. His round, boyish face and large, soft eyes were in striking contrast to the hard and cunning expressions of his two companions.

All three men were armed with long Shan swords.

"This sapphire is no good at all", said Chong Soo; it is full of flaws and of a very dull colour too. What use is it to me? I was told that you had found a large stone, a good stone, Ai Seng. Where is it? Surely this miserable specimen is not the stone you dug up yesterday, and hid so quickly in your belt."

Ai Seng looked uncomfortable.

"Who told you that; it is not true," he said quickly.

"I know, I know. You cannot find a big stone without my knowing, and you cannot sell little stones to me when you have a big one in your belt. Come on! Out with it!"

"I didn't bring it with me. I left it in charge of another man."

"Oh, then it's true that you found it, after all. That was one lie. Maybe you are lying again when you say you did not bring it with you."

"No, that is true, really true."

Sang Hla now joined in.

"Let me see that sword of yours. I want to get one like it."

Ai Seng began to look frightened.

"I will not let you see my sword, and I have no better stone than the one your father is holding."

Sang Hla drew his sword. "Show me that stone," he snarled, "the big one."

Ai Seng quickly drew his sword, jumped to his feet and made for the door. But he was too late. Sang Hla was there

97

before him and stood with his back to the door. The unfortunate lad was caught like a rat in a trap.

"Let me go," he cried, "let me go home, and I promise you I will bring the big sapphire and give it to you."

"Give it to me now," said the older ruffian. "It is in your belt."

"I won't give it," shouted poor Ai Seng in desperation; "get away from that door, or I will kill you, you thief. I am not afraid of you."

Brandishing his sword, he made for the door. But before he had taken two steps, Chong Soo leapt upon him from behind, and dealt him a smashing blow upon the head. Ai Seng staggered forward, blind with blood. Blow after blow was showered upon him. A fury seemed to have seized the old man and his son. Not until Ai Seng was a mere mass of hacked and bleeding flesh did they desist.

"Enough," said Chong Soo, "take off his belt."

His son knelt down and removed the wet and crimson-stained cloth which was bound round the unhappy boy's waist. A little pocket was sewn into one side of it, wherein was a tiny canvas bag.

The old man snatched the canvas bag, hurriedly pulled it open, and emptied its contents onto the palm of his hand.

There was the big sapphire, sure enough. An irregular lump of dull, unpolished blue, about the size of a large cherry. For years and years no such treasure had been found at Pailin. There, lying compact upon his bloodstained palm, was independence, wealth, idleness, unlimited vice, everything for which his rotten soul hankered, all in a neat little blue lump.

"We will leave tomorrow morning before daylight," he said. "We can get to Chantaboon in two days, just in time to catch the steamer to Bangkok. We will go on to Calcutta and sell the sapphire there. Nobody need ever know how we got it. Who knew that Ai Seng was coming here tonight? Who besides myself saw him find the sapphire? Come, let us wash away the blood, and then take this carrion out and bury it."

Ai Seng lay soaked with blood and quite still, but up to that moment a faint flicker of life still lingered in his body.

As the two murderers lifted him up, that faint flicker was extinguished.

At the same moment another event occurred in the hut which may not seem to be of great importance, but which was fated to be of some moment to one at least of the murderers.

A feeble squeak, which passed unheeded, was uttered in the thatch of the roof. It was the cry of a little mother mouse, who was then in the act of bringing into the world the first of a litter of six young mice. As Ai Seng gave his last dying gasp, the eldest of the young mice drew his first feeble breath.

II

Ai Seng's body was buried. The blood was washed away from the hands of his slayers and from the floor of the hut. Chong Soo and Sang Hla lay down on their sleeping mats to wait for the dawn, but neither of them slept much. Chong Soo spent much of the night wandering about the hut in the darkness.

Presently Chong Soo coughed. His son started

"Why do you not sleep Father," he asked.

"I cannot sleep, my son, nor can you. We shall never sleep in peace so long as we remain together. The sapphire from Ai Seng's belt is now in mine. You, too, have a little pocket in your belt. If I sleep, maybe I shall never wake again, and the sapphire will have a new hiding-place."

Sang Hla laughed hoarsely.

"You know me, father, but I know you too. You have got the sapphire. All I ask is my share. If I sleep, shall I wake to claim it?"

Thus did they pass the night — each on guard against the other. When dawn was near, they hurriedly gathered together their possessions, each strapped to his waist a little basket of cooked rice and condiments, and before the first gleam of daylight they had set forth on their journey to Chantaboon.

To say that they were afraid would be but a mild description of their state of mind. Every sound caused them to start, every shadow made them tremble. But it was not any stirring of their warped and hardened consciences that made them such cowards; nor did they fear pursuit. Murder was nothing new to them, robbery but a trivial incident. Ai Seng might not be missed for days. It might never be known that he had visited their hut; he might be thought to have left along with them.

No, it was fear of one another which possessed them both. Each of them, father and son, felt that at any moment he might be ruthlessly attacked and butchered by the other. Chong Soo's terror was even greater than that of his son. He was an old man, and knew that, if suddenly attacked, his chances of successful resistance were not good. But he derived a certain degree of inward satisfaction from the reflection that if he could manage to kill his son, the sapphire would be his; whereas, if he himself were the victim, his son would gain nothing; for during the night he had, while wandering around the hut, cunningly concealed the sapphire in a place where he thought nobody was likely to find it.

Sang Hla, on the other hand, was at least possessed of the comforting knowledge that he was much stronger than his father. But he was a coward, and as such feared even an encounter where his chances of success were without doubt good.

Fortune, or the powers of evil, favoured the younger man.

They were crossing one of the numerous streams which intersect that road, a stream some two feet deep and filled with slippery stones. With cat-like tread they picked their steps. Suddenly the old man slipped. He had put one foot on a slimy stone, and in trying to steady himself his other foot went into a hole in the bed of the stream. He stumbled forward and fell with his hands in the water.

Instantly, without a moment's warning or preparation, his son's knife entered his back with vicious thrust. One hoarse shriek, one foul oath, and the older rascal rolled over in the stream and started to float down with the current.

Sang Hla laughed. "That was good of you, father," he cried, "that was very good of you, to let me kill you in a place where no trace of blood will ever be seen. But do not float away and leave me."

100

He splashed after the half-dead man and seized him by the foot. Another couple of stabs completed the work, and then he started down the stream, dragging the corps with him.

A couple of bends along that jungle waterway, and he was as far from human ken as he would have been had he walked fifty miles. Three minutes walk from almost any forest path in Thailand, and one may well have reached a spot where no human foot will tread for years.

Feverishly he searched the body. Again and again he examined every bit of rag. He unfastened the old man's long hair and ran his fingers through its matted tresses. But no sapphire could he find. A Shan's wardrobe is scanty. Five minutes' search brought absolute certainty. The sapphire was not there.

Where had Chong Soo hidden it? Had he left it in the hut, to return for it secretly. Had he dropped it in the forest? Had it fallen from his clothes into the stream?

Sang Hla could find no answer to any of these questions. To search the forest and the stream, however, would have been a hopeless task. He decided to return to Pailin. He dragged his father's body a few yards back from the stream, gave it a parting kick, and in a minute or two was back again on the pathway.

He entered the village by a small lane at the back of his hut, meeting nobody by the way, slipped in unobserved, and flung himself down for his long-deferred sleep

At about ten he got up and went around the village asking whether anyone had seen his father. The old man had, it seemed, vanished in the night and — strange to say — Ai Seng was also missing.

In a place where every man, woman and child is engaged in the search for wealth, people do not trouble themselves much about their neighbours' business, nor worry greatly over their goings and comings. A week's gossip, a memory for a month, and Chong Soo and Ai Seng were forgotten.

III.

Never, I feel sure, has any building been subjected to so thorough a search as was the hut of Sang Hla. He could not rid himself of the idea that the sapphire was concealed somewhere about the place. When, at the dawn of each day, his neighbours took their spades and baskets and set out every man for his own digging, Sang Hla remained at home and spent hours engaged in a fruitless and infuriating hunt. Beneath the bamboo floor, above the grass-thatched roof, in every chink of the walls, he sought and sought again, refusing to be convinced that the quest was hopeless. Somehow he could actlally *feel* that the sapphire was somewhere near.

Now and then a neighbour came in and disturbed him at his rummaging, offering to assist him to find whatever was missing. But Sang Hla's angry growl and threatening frown did not tempt to a renewal of the offer. He was a nasty man to quarrel with.

He reproached himself bitterly with having killed his fathei. Far, indeed, was he from repenting that deed merely as being evil, or from feeling what we call remorse; but the old man had been useful in many ways and it was dull living alone. Besides, had he trusted Chong Soo, he might have had, after all, a half share in the spoil, or, better still, have found a more suitable opportunity to obtain the sapphire without risk of failure.

At last he started to dream, and his dreams filled him with a strange fear. Always, as he dreamed, he knew in his heart that the sapphire was somewhere near him, yet always there was some vague but relentless force which stood between him and the stone and prevented him from touching it. What threatened him he did not know, but it was something remorseless and determined. Sometimes, just as he was waking, he thought he felt a soft touch on his face and lips, and on those occasions his fear was so great that he remained still and helpless for some minutes after opening his eyes.

Finally he took to drinking. At first just a few drops of samshu to cheer him up, then more and more, but never enough to make himself helplessly drunk.

One night he woke suddenly, feeling on his lips the gentle touch he so feared and hated, and grabbed feverishly at his face. Something crept away and vanished in the darkness. He struck a light. There was nothing there.

A sickening fear, a mad dread overcame him. He grasped the samshu jar and drank again and again. Ah, now he felt better. He relinquished unknowingly the grim determination and set will which had dominated him for weeks. His firm-set jaw relaxed.

Still he drank, till at last he fell back in a state of help-less, slobbering drunkenness, and forgot all his fears in noisy slumber.

Hardly had he begun to snore when a tiny mouse crept from a hole in the bamboo flooring and ran quickly across the sleeping-mat. In less than a moment it had climbed the sleeper's body and was perched on his face. In its mouth it held, gently pressed between its teeth, a large red berry.

The mouse was trembling with excitement and squeaking from emotion. For weeks and weeks it had been watching and waiting, but never before had it found that wide-gaping slobbering mouth all ready to receive its gift. Night after night it had tried to press the berry between close-locked lips. but tonight the samshu had lent its aid, and the task was easy. With a final squeak of joy, the mouse dropped the berry into that yawning mouth.

Sang Hla gave an involuntary gulp, closed his lips, and swallowed the berry.

The little mouse seemed almost mad with excitement. It tore up and down over Sang Hla's prostrate form and then ran and leapt wildly about on the mat. Finally it climbed to a rafter above, and sat there watching.

Half an hour went by without anything happening. The mouse showed signs of impatience.

At last Sang Hla stirred in his sleep. He turned over onto his stomach, and curled himself up against his blanket. Then he groaned. Soon the hut was in a wild state of con-fusion. Sang Hla was rolling on the floor in agony, cursing and yelling like a lunatic. His screams brought in his nearest neighbours. The local medicine man was quickly on the scene. But the symptoms baffled everybody. Nor could the patient give any explanation.

For three hours Sang Hla lay there writhing, his fingers twitching, his eyes rolling. Then his struggles grew less, and he lay in a seeming stupor.

103

Suddenly the bystanders saw him raise his eyes and stare with a look of terror at the rafter above him. His eyes became fixed and glazed and his body stiff. Then, with a bursting sound, as though the words were forced from him, he yelled:— "Ai Seng, Ai Seng!"

The watchers followed his gaze to the rafter, the sight of which seemed to cause him such fear; but there was nothing there save a tiny mouse.

A second later, Sang Hla closed his eyes and was silent. It was the silence of death.

*　　*　　*

Unnoticed by any of the people present, the little mouse, with many excited squeaks, ran quickly among the rafter and through a hole in the thatch of the roof. The boughs of a spreading tamarind tree which overshadowed the hut, hung down and here and there touched the roof. The mouse leapt onto the nearest bough and ran along it to the trunk of the tree. There, some twenty feet from the ground, was a small hole, leading to a hollow space in the tree — the mouse's home. It crept inside, worn out by its long vigil, and sought its nest

But the mouse, though mateless, had a companion in its retreat. As it lay there at rest, it was not alone. It was nestling against a hard; bright object, rough yet transparent, and of a rich blue colour — the sapphire of Ai Seng.

CREDIT BALANCE

Extracts from the "Morning Sentinel," an English language newspaper published in Bangkok, Siam.

June 24th, 1953.

Disappearance of Japanese business man.

On the arrival of the Northern Express at Den Jaya at about 7 a.m. on the morning of June 22nd, Mr. K. Isonaga,

Manager of the Shimidzu Steel Company, reported to the station Police that another Japanese passenger, Mr. Manjiro Kasaki, of the Commercial Bank of Shimidzu, was missing from the train.

It appears that Mr. Kasaki and Mr. Isonaga, after leaving Bangkok at 6 p.m., had dinner on the train with an English passenger, Mr. J. L. Nixon of the Papuan Oil Syndicate. After dinner, they sat up talking until about 11 p.m., when they all went to their cabins. Mr. Kasaki and Mr. Nixon shared a cabin together, Mr. Nixon occupying the upper, and Mr. Kasaki the lower berth. At about 6. the next morning Mr Isonaga went to Mr. Kasaki's cabin to tell him that the train would soon be arriving at Den Jaya, their destination. Mr. Kasaki was not in his berth, and a search of the train failed to discover him. Mr Nixon stated that shortly after the train left Pitsanuloke at 2.45 a.m. Mr. Kasaki got up and turned on the light. This woke Mr. Nixon, who asked Mr. Kasaki what he was doing. The latter replied that he could not sleep, and was going to the restaurant car to get some iced water. He then turned out the light and left the cabin. Mr. Nixon went to sleep, and did not wake again until about 6 a.m., when Mr. Isonaga came to the cabin to call his friend.

Telephone messages to all the stations between Den Jaya and Pitsanuloke failed to produce any information as to the whereabouts of the missing man.

————————

July 1st, 1953.

It is reported from Pitsanuloke that the body of a man, wearing pyjamas, has been found on a sandbank in the Menam River, about six kilometres North of Pitsanuloke. The body had been mutilated by vultures to such an extent as to render definite identification impossible, but what remained of the pyjamas corresponded with the description given to the Police of those worn by Mr. Kasaki at the time of his disappearance from the express on June 23rd last.

A correspondent of the "Sentinel" interviewed Mr. J. L. Nixon, who appears to be the last person who saw Mr. Kasaki alive. Mr. Nixon stated that he had invited Mr. Kasaki and his friend Mr. Isonaga to dine with him, and had sat in the restaurant car talking to them until about 11 p.m. Both the Japanese gentlemen had a few drinks, but neither was intoxicated. Mr. Kasaki took a glass of iced water to the cabin with him. After drinking this, he undressed and went to sleep in the lower bunk. Mr. Nixon climbed into the upper bunk and soon fell asleep. Soon after the train left Pitsanuloke, he was awakened by Mr. Kasaki getting up and turning on the light. On being asked what he was doing, Mr Kasaki said he did not feel well, and was going along to the restaurant car to get another glass of iced water. Mr. Nixon then went to sleep again, and did not wake until about six, when Mr. Isonaga came to the cabin to rouse his friend. Mr. Nixon is not sure of the exact time when Mr. Kasaki left the cabin, but suggests that perhaps it may have been shortly before the train crossed the bridge over the Me Yome River at Ban Dara. Mr. Kasaki, who complained of feeling unwell, may have stood on the step of the carriage in order to get some fresh air, overbalanced, and fallen into the river. As the body which is presumed to be that of Mr. Kasaki was found on a sandbank some kilometres South of the Ban Dara bridge, this appears to be the most probable explanation of the matter.

July 7th, 1954.

Our readers will recall the strange occurrence on the Northern Express in June of last year, when a Japanese business man named Manjiro Kasaki was reported to have disappeared, and the discovery, a few days later, of a body, presumed to be that of the missing man, on a sandbank in the Menam River. We are now in a position to publish a true explanation of this affair, which our readers will, we are sure, agree with us in considering to be not only astonishing, but dramatic in the highest degree.

It will be remembered that Mr. J. L. Nixon, who shared Mr. Kasaki's cabin at the time of his disappearance, died, some three months ago, after an operation for cancer. It appears that Mr. Nixon, before entering the Nursing Home for the operation which proved fatal, deposited with a friend a sealed envelope, which, in the event of Mr. Nixon's death, was to be delivered three months later to the Editor of this paper. The envelope contained as MS signed by Mr. Nixon, which we reproduce verbatim.

Bangkok, April 4th, 1954.

This is a true statement by me, John Lumley Nixon, Assistant Manager of the Papuan Oil Syndicate Ltd., of Bangkok, Siam, concerning the death of Mr. Manjiro Kasaki, of the Commercial Bank of Shimidzu, Japan, on June 23rd, 1953.

At the time of the outbreak of World War II, I and my younger brother, Edward James Nixon, were both employed by the Kuala Locheng Tin Company, Perak, Federated Malay States. I was then aged 24 and my brother was 21. On the outbreak of war, we both enlisted in the Perak Volunteers. When the Japanese invaded Malaya in December, 1941, we were both called up for service. Our regiment, with the rest of the British Army in Malaya, was gradually forced back onto the island of Singapore, and we were among the 160,000 British and Indian prisoners captured by the Japanese when that city fell in February 1942.

My brother and I were among the unfortunate ones who were sent to Southern Siam to work on what has rightly been called the "Death Railway" between Siam and Burma. The barbarous treatment we received is well known, and is attested by the appalling death rate among the railway workers, and the pitiable condition of the survivors when the Japanese were forced to surrender in August 1945.

On the morning of June 23rd, 1943, my brother Edward and I were among a party of forty men sent out from the camp at Ban Luk to fell trees for railway sleepers on a section of the railway about six miles from the camp. My brother was ill with malaria, and begged to be left behind, but the Japanese Captain in charge of the camp insisted on his accompanying us. We had a guard of five Japanese soldiers, under the command of Sergeant Manjiro Kasaki. After we had gone for less than a mile, my brother fell down, saying

107

that he could go no farther. Sergeant Kasaki kicked him, and beat him with the butt end of his rifle. My brother got up, but after staggering for a few paces, fell down again. Then Sergeant Kasaki said:— "I cannot spare a man to watch over this fellow. Dig a hole in that sandbank." A hole was dug, and my young brother was carried and put into it, after which the Japanese soldiers filled it in with sand, leaving only my brother's head and shoulders sticking up out of the sandbank. When I protested I was kicked and beaten, and forced to go on to work with the other 38 men.

Eight hours later, on our way back to the camp, we came once more to the sandbank. "Dig the fellow out!" shouted the Sergeant. We dug him out. He was still alive, and able to recognise me. He whispered to me:— "Johnny, do not forget." Then he died, and we buried him there in the sandbank. But I bore his words in my mind, and I did not forget.

After the war, I got a job in the Bangkok Office of the Papuan Oil Syndicate, and on June 22nd, 1953, exactly ten years after the murder of my brother Edward, I found myself mounting the Northern Express for a visit to Chiengmai on my firm's business. The first person I saw on the train was Sergeant Kasaki. I knew him at once, but he did not recognise me. When he killed my younger brother, I was a walking skeleton, and wore a beard. In 1953 I was inclined to be stout and ruddy, and was clean-shaven.

On looking at the label on my cabin door, I found, to my great satisfaction, that my stable companion was to be none other than Sergeant Kasaki, and I made up my mind there and then that he would never reach his destination. If I could kill him without being found out, so much the better. If not — well, my doctor had warned me that I was unlikely to live for more than a few years, and here was an opportunity of doing a good deed before the time came for me to depart.

I lost no time in scraping acquaintance with Kasaki and his friend Isonaga, and invited them to dinner with me. I stood them the best dinner we could get, and as much beer and whisky as they could swallow — and they were both fairly good performers in that line. After dinner, we set up drinking and joking until about eleven. I insisted on paying for everything, and I carefully noted that Kasaki's share, including dinner, totalled Ticals 82.75. I wanted to know exactly how I stood when my final account was made up.

When we returned to our cabin, Kasaki was more or less "merry" and Isonaga had taken so much that I felt sure he would not worry me for a few hours ahead. I waited until the train had left Pitsanuloke, and then quietly came down from my upper bunk, turned on the light, and sat on the folding stool close to the berth where Kasaki lay asleep. He was lying on his back — an ideal position for my purpose. For a few moments I hesistated. Then I remembered my young brother's head and shoulders sticking up out of the sandbank. I waited no longer, but seized Kasaki's throat in both my hands. For a moment he was conscious. He looked at me, and I felt that he remembered me. I am a strong man and it took me only a few seconds to sequeeze the life out of him. He did not make such noise — only a rather unpleasant gurgling sound, but the rattling of the train and the echoes of the night were so loud that I felt sure nobody would hear him.

When I was certain he was dead, I turned out the light, opened the window alongside the bunk, and kept the body balanced on the window's edge. I had made the journey several times before, and knew that in a short time we should be crossing the Me Yome River near Ban Dara. A few minutes later, the changed sound of the wheels showed me that we were on the bridge. As soon as I judged that we were about half way across, I pushed the carcase out, shut the window, and went back to sleep.

At about six o'clock the next morning, Mr. Isonaga woke me up, saying that he had come to call his friend, but could not find him in the cabin, and asking me whether I had any idea where he could be found. I professed to be completely in the dark as to Kasaki's whereabouts.

This is a true and correct explanation of the disappearance of Mr. Manjiro Kasaki from the Northern Express.

When my final account is made up, if justice is done to me, it will be held that I have a cash balance standing to my credit. Kasaki's death merely balances the murder of my brother, but I have a right to be credited with a sum of Ticals 82.75 for food and drink supplied to his murderer.

(Signed)   JOHN L. NIXON.

*   *   *

WILL-O-THE-WISP

Some years ago, when motor roads in Thailand were few and bad, I was travelling by motor-bus to the town of Wiengchak. Just at dusk, we reached a small village named Ban Larp, about twelve miles short of our destination, when the 'bus developed two simultaneous punctures, and the driver gave up all hope of going any farther that night. It was important for me to go on to Wiengchak without delay, but there was no sort of transport to be found at Ban Larp — not even a bicycle However, somebody told me that by taking a short cut through the forest, it was possible to walk to Wiengchak in something over two hours. I therefore went to the house of the village Headman, and asked him whether he could find me a guide, as I wanted to walk to Wiengchak along the forest road.

The Headman, a white-headed old patriarch, seemed to be greatly upset by this suggestion, and replied that he was quite certain nobody in the village would be willing to go with me, no matter how much I offered to pay. I asked the reason, and he explained the matter by telling me the following story:—

Many years ago (said the old Headman) I and my son, Noi Lert, were called to Wiengchak by the District Officer to help put up a rest-house for the Crown Prince of Siam, who was making a tour of the North. It took us six days to complete the rest-house, and we were not paid off until late

110

in the evening of the sixth day. My son had recently married a very pretty girl, and was anxious to return home that same night. As for me, I wanted to wait till morning, as the journey by the main road would have taken us four hours, and the shorter track through the forest had a bad name; people were afraid to take that path after dark, as the forest was reputed to be haunted by those spirits known as *phi i-khoi,* which lure travellers to their destruction. I myself had never heard of anyone meeting the spirits, but maybe that was because nobody ever travelled that way after dark. Nevertheless, I was very unwilling to take the risk. However, Nai, you will easily understand that a young fellow twenty years af age, like my son Noi Lert, newly-wed, with a pretty wife waiting for him at home, is disinclined to worry about *phi i-khoi* or any other kind of spirits. In the end he talked me over, so off we set along the jungle path.

It was a moonlight night, so we had no difficulty in finding our way. Maybe we were a bit nervous at first, but we grew bolder as we strode along through the forest, and soon Noi Lert started to sing.

We had been walking for about an hour when suddenly we heard the sound of a bell — a small, tinkling bell it seemed to be — like those you see hanging on the edge of a temple roof. Very sweet it sounded, and we stopped to listen to it As we listened, we heard another sound, like somebody playing a flute, but the tune being played was different from any I had ever heard. My son then said that he wanted to leave the path and go off into the forest to find out who was responsible for the music. I objected to this, though in truth I was greatly attracted by the sound of the bell and the flute, and inwardly desired to seek out the player, whoever he might be. While we stood arguing there, somebody began to sing in the forest. I cannot say whether it was the voice of a man or a woman. All I can say is that it was incredibly sweet, and filled me with delight — yet at the same time I was overcome by a feeling of intense fear.

After listening to the voice for a few moments, Noi Lert and I seemed to lose all control over ourselves. Without more ado, we dashed away into the dark forest, looking neither to the right nor the left, intent only on following the music and the singing.

Soon we came to a deep stream flowing below us along a rocky ravine. Noi Lert, more active than I, scrambled down the side of the ravine, and was across the stream in a few moments. I, less agile, slipped and fell down the incline, and the next thing I knew was that I was lying in the bed of the stream with a broken leg. Vainly I called to Noi Lert to come back to help me. Lured on by the music and the voice, he rushed forward madly through the undergrowth. There I lay helpless, and in a few minutes I ceased to hear the sound of Noi Lert's trampling, and the sounds which had drawn us on likewise faded gradually away. All was silent in the forest.

So there I lay moaning in the bed of the stream until daylight came. Then I slowly managed to drag myself back to the footpath, where I waited until after midday, when a party of six villagers came along. I told them what had happened to my son and myself. Two of them started to make a rough stretcher of fallen branches to carry me back to the village, and while they were at work the other four went into the forest to search for Noi Lert.

More than an hour passed by before they came back, bearing the dead body of my son, and related to us how they had found him. They had, they said, easily traced his path by the broken twigs and crushed undergrowth which marked his frantic onrush through the forest. At last, in a little open clearing, they came upon a great heap of jungle flowers — flowers of every colour, red, blue, white, purple and yellow, all piled up together; and under the heap of flowers lay my son, Noi Lert. He looked quite peaceful, and had a smile on his lips, so that at first they thought he was sleeping. But he was dead. The *phi i-khoi* had enticed him away with their music and their singing, and had taken his spirit to wander forever with them in the forest.

Did you like my story, Nai? Did it interest you? If it did, I ask one thing of you as a reward. Do not travel by the forest path tonight.

*   *   *

LAMYAI GIRL

In Northern Thailand, July is lamyai* month. Early in the month the lamyai fruit ripens, and a large part of the population is engaged in picking and packing the little white fruit with the hard brown shell, ready for export by rail to Bangkok.

In Chiengmai, young men who are good climbers are in great demand during the lamyai season. Lamyai picking ranks as skilled labour, and a good picker earns high pay. Many young fellows try to get leave from their regular jobs for the sake of the money they can earn by climbing a high pole and spending their days among the branches of the lamyai trees.

Women and girls stand beneath the trees to collect the fruit as it is passed down to them, and to pack it in large baskets for despatch to the railway station. A great deal of friendly badinage may always be heard between the young men up the trees and the maidens down below, and many a romance is started in the month of July. August, it is said, is the month when the marriage rate is the highest in the year.

Kam Nuan was an orphan girl aged sixteen. Born in Bangkok, she had come up North to Chiengmai on an excursion train with her parents, to attend the water festival which marks the Northern New Year in the month of April. Both her parents contracted malaria and died. Thus she found herself stranded, with no friends and no money, in a strange city. She had, however, a little gold neck-chain. Somebody told her that there was an old Lao Princess in a village a few miles from the city, who owned a large lamyai garden, and who was usually ready to pay a fair price for gold ornaments.

So Kam Nuan went to see the Old Princess. The old lady, hearing her sad story, felt sorry for her, and said:—

"Do not sell your little chain, if it is your only property. There is no need for you to starve. Stay here with me and help to look after my house. I will feed you and pay you a small wage. Later on, if you are unhappy here in Chiengmai, I will help you to return to Bangkok."

* Nephilium Longana or longan.

So Kam Nuan stayed on and became maid-of-all-work to the Old Princess.

When the lamyai season started in July, Kam Nuan asked the Old Princess to arrange with the Chinese merchant who had contracted to buy that year's crop, for her to work for the season as one of his packers, so that she could earn a little extra money. The Old Princess readily agreed, so one day in July Kam Nuan found hirself, together with three or four of the village girls, standing beside a large basket under a lamyai tree, waiting for the young fellow above to send down a supply of fruit.

*   *   *

Sri Butr was a young man of nineteen. His father, a fairly well-to-do farmer, lived next door to the Old Princess. His mother had died when he was a very small boy, and his step-mother, who had a daughter older than himself, was an ill-tempered and parsimonious woman. Nor was her daughter any more agreeable.

Sri Butr's ambition was to be a motor-driver, but it costs several hundred bahts to take driving lessons and pay other expenses incidental to becoming a licensed driver. His step-mother grudged every stang spent on him, and his father, who was an easy-going man, had long since ceased to argue with his "better half." So Sri Butr had to make the best of things, and took on a job as ticket-boy on a motor-bus running between Chiengmai and Raheng, eighty miles to the South. A ticket-boy is looked upon in Chiengmai as a very inferior sort of being as compared with a driver. He has to lift heavy baggage up and down all day, and to engage in constant arguments, and now and then fights, with the more truculent passengers. The aim of every ticket-boy is to become a driver, so he usually manages, by hook or by crook, to take driving lessons whenever possible, and to save, if he can, the money necessary to elevate himself to that dizzy eminence.

Sri Butr was a good climber, so for two years past he had obtained leave of absence from his job during the month of July, in order to earn quintuple pay as a lamyai picker.

114

So one day Sri Butr found himself balanced precariously on top of a long bamboo, letting down bunches of fruit in a small basket to a girl who stood beneath the tree.

The Chinese contractor, keen on making the largest possible profit, had provided an outfit of bamboo ladders, basket and ropes which had been in use for several years. It thus happened that before long the rope by which Sri Butr was lowering the fruit, broke and the basket fell down, grazing the shoulder of Kam Nuan — for she it was.

"Sorry!" called out Sri Butr, "I hope it did not hurt you. I couldn't help it!"

"I'm all right, thanks," came back the answer.

Sri Butr was surprised to hear the lamyai girl speak with a Southern accent, as all the lamyai girls he had ever met were daughters of people in the neighbourhood. Later in the morning, when work stopped for the pickers and the girls to have their breakfast, he went to Kam Nuan and said:— "I am glad you were not hurt when the basket fell. I can hear from your accent that you come from the South. How does it happen that you are working as a lamyai girl here in Chiengmai?"

So Kam Nuan told him briefly the short story of her life. He was very sympathetic — maybe all the more so because she was an unusually pretty girl — and as the days passed by he got into the habit of sitting and talking to her during the intervals between work. Nobody took much notice of them, as most of the unmarried pickers were making love to the lamyai girls, some with, some without, serious intentions

Towards the end of the month, when the last few bunches of fruit were being garnered, Sri Butr said, "Kam Nuan, I am only a ticket-boy on a bus, drawing very small pay, but I hope to be a driver some day. While we have been working here together I have learnt to love you. Will you marry me? I must warn you that my step-mother and her daughter are rather disagreeable people, but my father is kind, and I will do my best to make you happy if you will trust yourself to me."

Kam Nuan, who had been greatly attracted from first by the tall, good-looking lad, did not waste much time before agreeing to Sri Butr's proposal, so off he went to break the news to his father and step-mother.

His father had for some time been cherishing a plan to marry Sri Butr to the daughter of the village headman, so was not particularly pleased to hear that his son had fallen in love with a girl who was not only penniless, but was a stranger from the South.

His step-mother, however, viewed the matter from quite a different standpoint. She said to herself:— "If Sri Butr marries the headman's daughter, we shall have to pay a substantial sum to the girl's parents, and give an expensive wedding feast to all the neighbours. Then, if the girl comes to live here, she will presume on the fact that her father is an important man to thwart and defy me. Moreover, they will certainly insist on the marriage being registered in the District Office under the new-fangled law, so we shall never be able to get rid of her except by expensive legal proceedings. If, on the other hand, he marries this miserable lamyai girl, no formal ceremony will be called for, and I shall get a servant-girl for nothing but her keep. If I get tired of her, I will manage to get rid of her without any legal fuss."

Holding these opinions, she spoke out strongly in favour of letting Sri Butr marry Kam Nuan. Her husband, as usual, gave way in a very short time, so before long Kam Nuan bade farewell to the Old Princess, and found herself installed in the house next door as the wife of Sri Butr.

Alas! The high hopes which had filled Kam Nuan's heart when Sri Butr declared his love for her were fated to prove deceptive. Sri Butr adored her, and when he was in the house his step-mother and step-sister treated her fairly kindly. True, they made her do all the housework and draw water from the well, but they were at least civil to her. The old man, too, was always kind to her, but she soon discovered that he was a mere cypher in the house.

Unfortunately, however, Sri Butr was very often absent from home. The bus on which he was employed was garaged every second night at Raheng. Moreover, it was sometimes chartered for special trips to towns even farther South, and when this happened, Sri Butr might well be away from home for three or four nights, or even a week. As soon as his back was turned, his step-mother began at once to vent her spite against Kam Nuan, calling her a useless, lazy slut, a pauper lamyai girl, an intruder from the South, and so on, until the poor girl's life became a misery to her. When Sri Butr came back, she did not like to complain to him, as is only made him unhappy, and she knew he was too poor to take her away to live somewhere else, unless his father was ready to make him an allowance, which his step-mother would never permit.

Four months went by in this way. Then Kam Nuan found that she was going to have a baby. She did not dare to tell anyone about it, knowing that her husband's step-mother and step-sister would be furious. However, the sharp eyes of her mother-in-law did not fail to notice when she began to suffer from morning sickness, and to show other signs of pregnancy. One night, when Sri Butr had been absent for several days, the older woman taxed her with it.

Kam Nuan had to admit that the accusation was true. She was pregnant.

Then her mother-in-law broke out into an angry tirade.

"You useless, miserable creature. We have been keeping and feeding you all these months, hoping that in time you might learn to be of some assistance to me in the house. And just when I was beginning to drive a little sense into your empty head, you needs must have a baby! Just think what heavy expenses you will make us incur! You will be unable to work for months. And even when you are all right, we shall have to bring up your infant. Sri Butr is as bad as you are. He has no right to have a baby. He cannot support it. He cannot even support you."

To herself she thought:— "And here is another claimant coming along to filch away part of my husband's estate when he dies!"

*   *   *

Kam Nuan answered not a word. What could she say? She did not know when Sri Butr would be back. She had no friends in Chiengmai. Even the Old Princess was away — absent on a visit to Chiengrai.

117

Sorrowfully Kam Nuan went down from the house, and walked slowly across to the Old Princess's lamyai garden. Creeping quietly along among the trees, she came to the river.

"River, river," she whispered, "I am a poor lamyai girl, with no parents or friends. My husband is good, but I am only a burden to him. His people hate me, and in time he will follow their example, and hate me too. Now I am going to have a baby, and they will hate me even more. Let me come, with the tiny baby in my womb, to sleep beneath your quiet waters, and forget it all."

Suddenly she heard a vioce behind her. "Kam Nuan, what are you doing here? I have just come back from Raheng, and could not find you in the house. Then my step-sister said you had come this way. Why are you standing all alone by the river?"

Then Kam Nuan broke down, and told him all her troubles, how she had been over-worked and abused, and how she was going to have a baby, and would only be a trouble to him for ever. "I was only a poor lamyai girl," she said, "and you ought never to have married me. Many rich girls would have been glad to take you for a husband."

Sri Butr was horrified. "I never knew," he cried, that you had to bear such a load of misery, though I could see that my step-mother and her daughter did not like you much. I am filled with happiness to know that we are going to have a child. And as for your being a poor lamyai girl, what am I but a poor ticket-boy? Or, anyhow, that is what I was when I married you. But tonight I have come back to tell you some wonderful news. I am a ticket-boy no longer, but a licensed driver. And more than that, I am a bus-owner! Last week I won a third prize of forty thousand bahts in the state lottery! I drew the money in Raheng, and nobody here knows anything about it. With part of my fortune I bought a motor-bus. I have passed my driver's examination and taken out a license. I drove back to Chiengmai in charge of my own bus. True, it is only a small bus and not very new, but it goes splendidly, anyhow. It has been chartered to return to Raheng this very night with twenty-five passengers, at thirty bahts a head. I have eight thousand bahts in my

Creeping quietly along among the trees, she came to the river.

pocket, and just think of all the profits we are going to make with my bus — *our* bus!"

"I will buy a little house in Raheng, and we will stay there together, with our baby when it comes. You shall have a servant to help you in the house, and nobody shall call you a poor lamyai girl. You are the wife of a rich bus-owner, and you shall wear a pair of diamond ear-rings. Let us get away now, this very minute. Our bus is just round the corner, with my ticket-boy in charge, at the petrol station, and all the twenty-five passengers waiting to start. Never mind your old clothes! I will buy you new ones in Raheng Let us not waste a moment. I will not say goodbye to my people, because they have not treated you well, but some day, when our child can walk, we will bring it to see my father and he will be proud of his grandchild. But now — off we go!"

Then, hand in hand, they left the lamyai garden where they had first met and walked along the lane, past the house of Sri Butr's father, and made their way to the waiting bus Three minutes later they were off on their journey to Raheng.

The bus creaked a little, rumbled slightly, and rattled quite a lot. The horn was wheezy, and the headlights none too bright, but its owner-driver and his little wife thought it was the finest bus in the world. They sang with joy as soon as they were under way; and all the twenty-five passengers, moved by their happy spirit, started to sing too.

*   *   *

And there let us bid them farewell, seated singing side by side on the front seat of their old bus, journeying southwards through the dark night

THE FIGHTING BEETLE

In Thailand, people are ready to risk their money on any sort of a fight. In ancient times, Kings thought nothing of

120

matching savage elephants against one another. Today, besides human boxers, we find fighting bulls, rams cocks, fishes and beetles.

The fighting rhinoceros beetle is a native of Northern Thailand, and in the provinces of Chiengmai and Lampang beetle contests are very popular, and large sums of money are often won and lost on these fights.

A rhinoceros beetle has two horns, one on its head, where a horn ought to be, and one on its thorax. The thorax horn is stationary, and the insect bites its opponent by bringing the head horn into contact with the thorax horn.

This is how beetles are made to fight. A long stick is prepared, in the middle of which there is a tiny, scooped-out prison chamber, shut by a tiny door, containing a tinier window. In this little prison a female beetle is placed, unapproachable, yet partly visible, and presumably smellable. The two pugilists are put onto the stick, and they fight for the lady. They are not always very keen, and sometimes have to be urged on by the use of little tin buzzers on sticks, which are twiddled near them to excite them. They rarely, if ever, inflict any visible wounds on one another, but when their bodies are well pinched, they give forth a loud hissing sound, which rather leads one to conclude that they do not like it. Their owners revive them, between the rounds, by spitting sugar-cane juice onto them, and sometimes by fanning them. If one of the beetles turns tail and will not come back, it is adjudged the loser. Sometimes, too, one contestant will seize the other between its horns, drag it by sheer force off the stick, and heave it bodily forth into the wide world. Occasionally, one of the beetles may lose a leg. When this happens, its fighting days are over.

The lady beetle has, I always think, a very thin time, cooped up in her tiny cell, while her rival suitors fight for her above her sky-light window. Neither victor nor vanquished is for her, anyhow, as love-making is held to be extremely bad for fighting beetles. A lot of money is staked on these fights, and the owner of a good beetle may make a small fortune out of it. But the poor beetle, after all its fighting and suffering, is not even allowed to snatch a hasty kiss.

To catch new fighting beetles, all one has to do is to hang out a stick of sugar-cane on the verandah at night. In the morning, during the proper season, there will often be a beetle or two browsing on the cane. You just slip a noose of cotton or twine round its horns, and there you are! To ensure the capture of really good beetles, a little magic is to be recommended.

Now I will tell you the story of a fighting beetle I once knew, his triumphs and his tragic fate.

I formerly had a servant named Kham Ai, a foolish, jolly fellow, and a great gambler. One day he came to me looking very dejected, and said that he wanted me to do him a great favour. I promised him to do anything I could, within reason, and he then proceeded as follows:—

"Nai, I am in great trouble. I have been backing horses at the Gymkhana Club races, and have had a terrible run of bad luck. I have lost all my money, sold my watch, and pawned my bicycle. But I see a wonderful chance of getting it all back. I have dreamed for three nights running that I was winning big sums of money by means of a wonderful fighting beetle, which you had caught by the use of a magic spell, you had presented to me. I therefore beg of you to put out a stick of sugar-cane tonight, first pronouncing over it a powerful foreign spell, and if you catch a beetle, to give it to me."

Of course I agreed to do this, and we at once prepared the necessary stick of sugar-cane. This I ceremoniously laid on top of my book of magic charm — known in England as Whittaker's Almanack — and at the same time solemnly repeated the following lines:—

> Little Jack Horner sat in a corner,
> Eating his Christmas pie.

This charm was successful. We hung out the cane that night, and in the morning, sure enough, there was a magnificent fighting beetle calmly grazing. I presented him to Kham Ai, at the same time suggesting that he should be named *Chaiya*, meaning "Victory."

Kham Ai was horrified, assuring me that to give the beetle such an arrogant name before he had proved his prowess was to court disaster. So he received the more modest appellation of *Chiphai* — meaning "Ruin."

A few days later "Ruin" was taken to a big beetle meeting, where he triumphantly overcame all his opponents. After this, he was permitted to bear the name of *Chaiya*.

"Victory" never once looked back. His career was a continuous blaze of glory.

In a few weeks, Kham Ai had redeemed his bicycle, bought a new watch, and was wearing a beautiful gold chain, with a sacred amulet attached. He also stood a big feed to his fellow-servants and most of the neighbours — minced pork, crab curry, vermicelli cakes, and unlimited rice liquor.

Alas! I can hardly bear to relate the sad end of this true story. "Victory" had been pursuing his triumphant career for about three months when he was matched to fight against a celebrated champion beetle from Lampang. A lot of money was staked on this contest. The battle was long and arduous. In the end, "Victory" managed to grasp the Lampang champion between his horns and cast him forth into the void. But in this moment of conquest, one of his hind legs became datached from his body. His fighting career was at an end.

A few days later I asked Kham Ai what he had done with "Victory". I was filled with shame and horror when he replied:— "I fried him last night, and ate him with spinach and chilli sauce; he tasted delicious!"

I completely failed to make Kham Ai see how terrible it was to fry and eat a creature which had helped him to redeem his bicycle from pawn, buy a new watch and a gold chain with a sacred amulet attached, and to gain a lot of money as well.

Almost like cannibalism, it seemed to me.

*   *   *

THE THIRD RIDER

The first time I visited Muang Fang, many years ago, I was told to go to see Sang Saw, the Shan Headman there, and to get him to tell me the story of the twisted elephant tail which hung on his wall.

Sang Saw was at that time a very old man, and it is now many years since he told me the story, so the events he related must have occurred at least a hundred years ago; and this is the tale he told me.

When I was a boy (said Sang Saw), there was a very savage elephant in the forest between Muang Fang and the frontier of Burma. It was a tuskless male, known here as a "Pu Sidaw," and it had a twisted tail, the very tail which you see hanging on my wall there. People said that it was invulnerable. It had killed two men. One of them was an elderly hunter, known as "Uncle Bald-Head", and the other was a young fellow with only one eye, named Ai Lat. Hunters who ventured into the forest to try to shoot this elephant all related that they had seen its two victims seated on its back. Old Bald-Head sat on its neck, with one-eyed Ai Lat behind him. This sight so terrified them that in every case they turned and fled from the forest without daring to shoot at the elephant.

My elder brother, Sang Keow, was a keen hunter. He made up his mind that he would try to kill the "ghost elephant", as it had come to be called. Our father did his best to dissuade him, but he would not listen, and at last one day he set forth for the forest, taking me with him. The only sort of fire-arms to be found in Muang Fang at that time were muzzle-loading, flint-lock guns. Bearing his old gun, and with me trotting at his heels, Sang Keow strode boldly through the forest.

*　　*　　*

Soon we struck the tracks of an elephant, which we followed for over an hour. Then we suddenly saw, coming through the undergrowth, the "ghost elephant," and, seated on its back, sure enough, were an elderly man with a bald head and a young fellow with only one eye! We were terrified at this sight, but my brother stood his ground, took steady aim, and fired at the elephant. I do not know whether he hit it, but it gave a bellow of fury and was upon him in an instant.

I could hear his bones cracking as it trampled him under foot. What could I do, Nai? Nothing! I was only a little

124

boy, and I had no weapon. I turned and ran. I ran on and on, never stopping until I reached my home.

My brother's death preyed on our father's mind so much that he almost became insane. He could do no work, but wept and moaned all day long. Moreover, he became in some way obsessed by the idea that I was to blame for what had happened. He seemed to hate me, and would often taunt me, saying that I was a coward to let my brother be killed by the "ghost elephant." But what could I have done, Nai?

So, as you may suppose, I led a very unhappy life. At last, when four years had gone by, and I had grown to be a man, I made up my mind that I would have a shot at the elephant which had killed my brother, even if it cost me my life. But first I went to Payao, where I had been told there was a very powerful magician. I sought him out, and asked him to prepare for me a magic bullet, able to penetrate the hide even of a supernatural elephant. He made me pay him all the money in my possession, and then he gave me a magic silver bullet, after having first pronounced over it a long incantation in a strange language.

*   *   *

When I returned home, I said nothing to my father, but the very next morning I loaded my old flint-lock gun with the magic silver bullet and set forth all alone for the forest. Everything happened exactly as it had done on the former occasion. I followed the elephant's track for a long time, until at last I heard it crashing about in the undergrowth. Then it came out, and once again I saw the form of old Uncle Bald-Head seated on its neck, with one-eyed Ai Lat behind him.

I took up a steady position and raised my gun. At that moment I saw the figure of yet a third man on the elephant's back, behind Ai Lat. I knew at once that it was my brother, Sang Keow. Raising himself up, he leant forward and pointed with his finger at a spot on the elephant's head exactly half-way between its eye and the hole of its ear. I did not hesitate for an instant. I pointed my gun at the spot shown to me by my brother and fired.

125

The elephant stumbled a few paces forward and then fell dead. The three men whom I had seen on its back vanished.

Nai, I think I went mad. I danced and shouted for joy. Then I jumped onto the elephant's body and stamped all over it with my feet. I hacked at its trunk and ears with my knife and spat into its eyes, for I was filled with a fierce hatred against the evil beast which had killed my brother. Then I cut off its twisted tail to take to my father.

When I reached my home, I said nothing to my father, but kneeling at his feet, I laid before him the twisted tail.

For the first time since my brother's death, my father smiled at me. He took up the tail, and said, "Well done, Ai Noi," using the pet name which I had not heard since I was a small child.

The next day he died.

So that, Nai, is the story of the twisted elephant tail which you see hanging there.

*   *   *

BLACKMAIL

To judge by some of the London Sunday newspapers, blackmailers seem to be fairly plentiful in England. We are always reading of the sufferings of their unfortunate victims, who are allowed to relate their indiscretions in Court under a merciful anonymity, as Mr. A. or Miss X.

When I was living in Bangkok during the early years of the century, I was often called upon to give advice concerning a large number of different matters. But I only once came across a case of blackmail — and that case was settled out of Court.

This is how it happened. A young Chinese British subject named Heng, who was a sort of clerk and general factotum to a rich old rice-mill owner, came along one evening to see me privately, and told me the following story.

A couple of months before Heng came to see me, his master had been absent on a visit to Singapore. His master's wife, who was quite a young woman, was taken ill one night, and called Heng into her bedroom at an early hour — this is what *he* said — to make tea for her. As he was coming out of the room, just before daybreak, he ran right into the arms of an old lady named Meh Puan, who was employed to do various odd jobs about the house. Later in the day, Meh Puan came to Heng and asked him to lend her fifty bahts, at that time worth about three Pounds. This was just the amount of Heng's monthly salary, and he told Meh Puan that he could not afford to let her have it. The old lady then said:—

"I am your true friend, and you know that I would never say anything which might get you into trouble. You had better lend me the money."

These words were spoken in pleasant tones, but the old lady had, so it seemed to Heng, a very nasty look in her eye as she said them, and Heng, without any further argument, went to his room and brought out fifty bahts to "lend" to her.

From that time onwards, Heng's life became a misery to him. Meh Puan kept on "borrowing" money from him about once a week. He had saved up four hundred bahts with the intention, later on, of starting a small shop. All that money was now in Meh Puan's hands, and he had to borrow more to satisfy her demands. Moreover, his mistress had also been victimized, and had been bled to an even greater extent than Heng himself. Ten times as much, he told me.

"Would it not be better to tell your master the whole story, and defy the old harpy?" I asked.

Heng turned pale. "You do not know my master so well as I do," he said; "he is a most jealous old man. He would never swallow my story about making tea in his wife's bedroom. Who would? Did you? He would divorce his wife, and would probably kill me as well."

I confessed to having been a trifle sceptical about the tea story, and told Heng to come and see me again in a few days. In the meanwhile, I would consult a friend of mine, a barrister, and ask him, if he could, to suggest some means whereby the unlucky Heng could extricate himself from the dilemma in in which he was placed.

The following Sunday morning, Heng came to see me again. I had no good news for him, as my friend had been able to suggest no other solution to the problem except that which I had made myself — confession. Poor Heng was very dejected, and said that only one thing remained for him to do, and that was to leave at once for his native city of Hong-kong, and never return to Siam. "And even then," said he, "my unfortunate mistress will have to bear this persecution until either she or old Meh Puan dies."

It so happened that I was myself in a very unhappy mood that morning, for I had just been forced to make away with a favourite dog, which had been run over by a tram and had two legs broken. I had obtained from a medical friend two capsules of cyanide — one as a reserve, in case the dog spat out the first. The dog was lying there dead when Heng came to see me, and the spare capsule was on my table. I told him what had happened. He seemed very interested, and enquired whether the capsule contained enough poison to kill a man. When I told him that there was enough in it to make an end of three or four men, he begged me to give it to him, saying that his mistress's little fluffy dog, (which I knew quite well) was very ill, all its hair coming out, unable to eat and slowly dying, so that it would be an act of mercy to put it out of its misery.

I ought to have been suspicious, as the idea of killing an animal from motives of mercy is by no means so familiar in the East as in the West; but at that time I was young and credulous, and Heng was such a mild and innocent-looking youth that I accepted his statement without question, and gave him the capsule, at the same time strictly enjoining him on no account to leave it lying about.

For a couple of months after that I saw and heard no more of Heng. Then, one evening, when I was taking a walk, I happened to pass not far from his master's rice-mill when I met him coming towards me. This was a new Heng. Gone was the anxious, hunted expression he had worn when I last saw him. He was bright and cheerful, and seemed full of confidence and assurance.

128

I asked him how things were going in regard to old Meh Puan and her "borrowings."

"Oh," said he, "that is all finished and done with. The old lady is dead. She died suddenly a few nights after I last saw you. She was all right in the evening, but in the morning there she lay dead in her bed. The Chinese doctor my mistress called in said she had had a heart attack. Of course, Meh Puan was very old, and no doubt her heart was weak. And just think! She had not spent a single cent of all the money my mistress and I had lent her. There it was, and more besides, in her box. So we were able to repay ourselves without any fuss, and there was enough left to give her a most beautiful cremation. She had no relations except one son, who lived at Paknam. He came up to Bangkok for the cremation, and wept with emotion when he realised how kindly my mistress and I had treated his mother, and saw what a lovely cremation we had given her."

Just then, along came Heng's mistress, followed by her little fluffy dog!

"Great Heavens!" I exclaimed, "Is not this the little dog you told me was dying, and which you intended to put out of its misery with the poison capsule I gave you?"

"Yes, Sir," replied Heng, "this is the very same dog; but when I got home that day it seemed to be better, and just then a friend came in who told me he had a wonderful sort of medicine for the treatment of all kinds of dog diseases. So we had another try at curing it, using my friend's medicine, and we succeeded; and here it is, alive and well, as you see."

"But the capsule!" I cried, "What about that? I hope you did not leave it lying about."

"Oh, no, Sir," replied Heng, "when I found I did not need it for the little dog, I got rid of it. I put it down the sewer."

What could I say or do?

I went home feeling uncomfortable, very uncomfortable. And even now, after fifty years have elapsed, and both Heng and his mistress are long since dead, I still feel at times a little bit uneasy about the death of old Meh Puan. However, when feelings of that sort assail me, I console myself with three reflections:—

Firstly. After all, what proof have I that the old lady did not in fact die of a heart attack, as diagnosed by the Chinese doctor?

Secondly. She was a very unpleasant old lady, anyhow.

Thirdly. They gave her a most beautiful cremation.

*   *   *

THE WATER ELEPHANT

"Do not follow that little stream," said the hermit; "true, there are some very fine mushrooms to be found along its banks. But it is not safe for young people like you to wander about there."

"But, Uncle," answered Noi Sawang, "my grandfather went there only last month, and brought back some magnificent mushrooms — and he never spoke of any danger; why cannot my wife and I go there too?"

Noi Sawang was a young farmer from the village at the foot of the mountain. He was twenty-two years of age, and his wife, Bua Kieng, was only seventeen. They had been married but a month. The padi-planting season was over, and they had come up the mountain to search for mushrooms, some to sell, some to flavour their curry. The old hermit dwelt in a small cave at the mouth of the little streamlet where Sawang's grandfather had reported the existence of a specially tasty species of mushroom. The hermit had lived there for thirty years, and was known throughout the country-side as the greatest authority on all matters relating to the mountain.

"Your grandfather is a very old man, my lad," said the hermit. "He must be nearly eighty. He ran very little risk. There is a water elephant living near that stream. It is a tiny creature, no larger than a rat, but formed exactly like a full-sized tusker. It has a lovely black, glossy skin, and little white ivory tusks. I saw it once, and it seemed to me be the most beautiful creature I had ever beheld. But I was safe enough.

I am old, very old, and your grandfather is even older than I. The water elephant takes no interest in aged people like us. It seeks only the souls of young people, to stay with it and keep it company in the forest, for it has no mate and no companions of its own kind, and often feels lonely. Last year two boy scouts came here to search for orchids. I warned them, as I am warning you, but they would not heed me. They went far along the stream, and collected hundreds of wonderful orchids. When they came back, they told me they had seen no sign of any water elephant; but only a week later one of them died quietly in his sleep. I am certain that the water elephant either cast its shadow on him, or else used its tiny tusks to stab his footprint in the sand at the side of the stream; in either case, he was doomed to die. Hearken to my words, and seek for your mushrooms in some other place."

Sawang was a well-educated young fellow. He had passed the Matayom Four examination, and his mind was full of modern learning and up-to date ideas. It seemed to him ridiculous to talk about an elephant the size of a rat, which could kill people by casting its shadow over them, or by stabbing their footprints with its tusk. He answered the old hermit politely, thanking him for his advice, but saying that he and his wife were ready to take the risk, and would take good care to keep well away from the water elephant and its shadow, should they chance to run across it.

So off they went along the little stream, laughing and singing. Soon their baskets were full of fine, succulent mushrooms. Then Sawang saw a huge purple orchid, high up on a forest tree. "Sit here on this mossy bank, little wife," he said, "and wait for me. I will climb up and pick that orchid. I know a *farang* who will pay me at least thirty bahts for it."

In a few minutes, Sawang was high up among the branches of the tree. He got his orchid, and then espied another on a higher bough. In the end, clambering from branch to branch, he collected five fine orchids. When he came down again, he found that Bua Kieng, tired of waiting so long, had fallen asleep on her mossy couch. "Wake up, wake up!" cried he, "We have at least two hundred bahts worth of mushrooms and archids! What a good thing it was that we did not let the old hermit scare us away with his stories about the water elephant. Of course, no such creature exists."

Soon they reached the hermit's cave, and Sawang said to the old man:— "Uncle, it was good of you to warn us about the water elephant; but, as you see, it did not injure either of us; so we are among the lucky ones, and maybe we will come here again in a week or so to collect more mushrooms and to climb the trees for orchids."

Then Bua Kieng said to the hermit:— "Uncle, I feel sleepy after walking so far. Let me lie down on the bamboo floor of your cave and doze for a few minutes." So saying, she lay down on the floor, using her arm as a pillow, and was soon fast asleep. Ten minutes later, Sawang called to her to get up, as they must go back home, to avoid being overtaken by darkness. She did not move. He shook her. She lay still, quite still. Then Sawang began to feel afraid. He felt her hands. They were cold. She had stopped breathing. She was dead.

Sawang knelt by her side, weeping:— "Uncle, Uncle," he wailed, "I was mad not to listen to your warning. The water elephant must have come while I was up that tree collecting orchids. The tiny, cruel water elephant has stolen her from me, and taken her to wander in the forest and cheer him up, along with the boy scout you told me about. I was mad, mad."

Next day, Sawang returned with some of his friends, and they carried back the body of his little wife to the village, and cremated it. And Sawang went back to live in his parent's house, a desolate, lonely young widower.

*   *   *

Days and weeks passed by, but Sawang did not forget. His heart was filled with feelings of rage against the water elephant, and he longed to be revenged upon the tiny animal which had stolen away his wife. At last he determined to kill it. He took his old flintlock gun, loaded it, and set forth for the mountain. When he reached the hermit's cave, the old man sought to dissuade him from going any further.

132

"You cannot shoot the water elephant," he said, "others have tried and failed — and they did not all return alive."

"Never mind," answered Sawang, "I will do my best to kill the devilish little creature, to avenge the death of my wife and the boy scout. I can at least have a shot at it, if I should chance to meet with it. As for myself, I do not care what happens to me. I have lost all interest in life."

So once again he set forth along the fateful streamlet, until he came to the place where he had left his wife sleeping on the former occasion, while he searched for orchids. Then he called out in a loud voice:— "Water elephant, come forth! Let me see you, wicked, cruel little beast, you who steal young people's souls to keep you company in your cursed forest. Come forth, and let me see you. I am not afraid of you. Come forth!"

There was a high, rocky boulder a few yards away from where Sawang stood. As he uttered these words, the little water elephant appeared on top of the boulder. It flapped its tiny ears, and swished its little tail, exactly like a full-sized elephant. Then it lifted its trunk as though in salutation. Sawang raised his gun. But he felt unable to shoot. As he stood there, pointing his gun at the water elephant, he felt all the rage and hatred in his heart melting away, and in their place he was filled with love and affection for the tiny, beautiful creature. He flung his gun to the ground, and knelt down with outstretched arms.

"Water elephant!" he cried out, "lovely, beautiful, kind-hearted little water elephant, I do not want to hurt you. I only want you to let me join my little wife, and wander forever with you in your lonely forest. Cast your shadow upon me, I beseech you, and let me stay here with you and my wife, and the boy scout. Have pity on me, and grant my request."

The rays of the setting sun shone through the trees, and cast the shadow of the little elephant upon Sawang's face as he uttered these words. Then he cried out:— "Water elephant, I will remain kneeling here until you are ready to take me. Do not make me wait too long."

*　　　*　　　*

133

As he uttered these words the little water elephant appeared on top of the boulder.

When night came on, and Sawang did not return, the old hermit took his lantern and went into the forest to search for him. There, by the side of the stream, he found him kneeling — dead. The water elephant had heard his petition.

THE PU-MIA

Luang Maitri, the Assistant Judge, had only just arrived in Chiengmai. This was his first appearance on the bench of a Northern Siamese Court, and he found some difficulty in following the evidence of the witnesses, many of whom, especially those from outlying villages, spoke only the Lao dialect.

It was a case of collision between a motor-bus and a bullock cart. The driver of the cart had just given his evidence.

"Call the next witness," ordered the Chief Judge.

"Nai Muang Chompu," cried the Court usher.

A smartly dressed young woman came forward and took her place in the witness box. She was wearing a pale blue costume, with high-heeled shoes. Her hair was fashionably "permed" and her complexion was too good to be true. Her manner, however, was modest and unaffected. She gave the impression of being a respectable girl of the working class, dressed up in her best cloths for the important task of giving evidence in Court.

"Surely there must be some mistake," said the Assistant Judge. "The Court called for 'Nai Muang' (Mr. Muang) but this is a woman."

"No, Your Honour," explained the usher. "There is no mistake. The witness is a pu-mia."

"A pu-mia!" exclaimed Luang Maitri; "What on earth is that?"

"A pu-mia is a man who always dresses like a woman," was the reply.

"But it is contempt of Court for a witness to come to give evidence wearing fancy dress," objected the young Judge, turning to his Chief, "Can we permit this sort of nonsense?"

"I think we had better go ahead with the case," replied the older man. "There are many queer things in Chieng-mai. We will talk it over when the case is finished."

So Nai Muang gave his evidence. He gave it clearly and well, but his manner throughout was not that of a young man, but of a well-behaved and modest young woman. Under cross-examination by the bus-owner's lawyer, he did not get rattled or upset, but stuck to his original statement. In short, his evidence was so convincing that when he had finished, the owner of the bus, after consulting his lawyer, asked the permission of the Court to compromise the case.

In giving permission for a compromise agreement to be made, the Chief Judge expressed his satisfaction at the manner in which Nai Muang had given his evidence.

On the way home after leaving the Court, the new Assistant Judge remarked:— "Mr. or Miss Muang Chompu, or whatever he, or she, is called, was certainly a model witness. But I still consider, with all due respect to your opinion, that if he is a man, he ought to have been sent home to change his clothes before being allowed to testify in Court."

"I think you are wrong," replied his Chief. "Northern Siam is not like Bangkok. I have never seen a respectable young man going about the capital dressed like a woman. But in Northern Siam there are a few so-called pu-mias in every district. This seems to be accepted as a normal thing. They are men, like you or me, but they insist on dressing like women, and object, as a rule, to doing a man's work, though ready enough to do laundry work, sewing or weaving, or to take on any job usually assigned to females. They do no harm, so far as I know, and nobody bothers about them. People say:— "He is a pu-mia," just as they might say of someone that he stutters, or is short-sighted, — and that is all there is to it. As for this particular "Pu-mia", I am rather surprised that you have not seen him before, as he is a near neighbour of yours. Of course you have been busy arranging your house since you arrived, but if you had been out into your garden, you would probably have seen Nai

136

Muang sitting in the lower verandah of the little wooden house next door to you, weaving silk skirts on a hand-loom. His father is dead, and he lives there with his mother and grandmother. The latter is a very old woman, in her dotage, and has been bedridden for years. Nai Muang's mother runs a small shop near by, and he himself does most of the house-work, as well as looking after the old lady."

Luang Maitri listened to all this with great interest. He was a student of human nature, and felt a special interest in the Lao people and their customs. In fact, he had specially asked the Minister of Justice to transfer him to Chiengmai for that very reason. He determined to make the acquaintance of Nai Muang.

The following evening, when Luang Maitri was walking in his garden, he observed Nai Muang, seated in the verandah of the little teak house next door, busily working at his loom. He was not quite so smartly dressed as when he appeared in Court, but his hair was nicely done, and a touch of powder and lipstick was evident.

"Good evening," said the Assistant Judge.

"Good evening, Sir," politely replied Nai Muang. "I hope you are comfortable in your new house, and do not find the Chiengmai winter too cold for you."

"I am geeting on very well, thank you. And now I want to ask you to do me a favour. I should like a few silk skirts to send to my sister in Bangkok. If you have any which you have not sold, could you bring them in to show me some day when you are not too busy?"

"Certainly, Sir, I will bring some tomorrow."

The following day being Sunday, when the Court was closed, Nai Muang came along to see his new neighbour, bringing with him a selection of silk skirts. The young Judge brought several of them. Then, after a little desultory conversation, he said:—

"When you were in Court the other day, you were summoned to give evidence under the name of Nai Muang Chompu, but you appear to be a girl. Excuse me for asking, but have you always dressed like that?"

"No, Sir," was the reply, "When I was small I had to go to school, and I was always dressed like a boy. I would have liked to dress as a girl, but my father, who was then alive, would not allow me to do so. I left school when I was fifteen, and my father then had me ordained as a Buddhist novice in the Lion Temple. I was there for two years. While I was in the temple, my father died, and I resigned from the temple in order to come home and help my mother. After I came home, I took to dressing and doing my hair like a woman. My mother did not object, so now I always wear feminine attire. I am doing very well, making and selling silk skirts, and sometimes I take in laundry too. I do all the cooking, and also look after my grandmother, who lies helpless in a room upstairs, and never comes down. My mother is busy all day in her shop. So, you see, we manage very well, and are better off than we should be if I tried to do a man's work, as I am not well-educated enough to get a highly paid job. Two years have passed in this way. I am now nineteen, and have come to look upon myself as a woman; moreover, all our neighbours accept me as such. I am very happy, now that I have become a woman. I do useful work and everybody is very kind to me. Moreover, I have much more liberty than is enjoyed by real girls whose parents are always fussing about them if they go out alone. You see, I am a woman with all the freedom of a man."

All this was said in a very simple, unaffected manner, which greatly impressed Luang Maitri. He had looked upon Nai Muang as a "freak," but after hearing him speak, he completely changed his opinion. Nai Muang now seemed to him to be merely a person whose manner of life was some-what exceptional.

As time went on, Nai Muang and his neighbour became very good friends. The educated man of the world was struck by the quickness and intelligence of the young Lao, and took an interest in teaching him history and world affairs, for his education had been somewhat rudimentary. Muang, for his part, taught the Judge the Lao dialect, which proved very useful to him in his work, and explained to him many local customs, which otherwise might have puzzled him. Twice a week, also, he came in to help with his neighbour's loundry, and took a hand with the cooking when guests were being entertained.

Luang Maitri owned a fox terrier named Tip, of which he was very fond. Muang took a great liking to this dog, and often brought it tit-bits of food which he had prepared at home.

One day, while Muang was busy over the washing-tub, the cry of "mad dog" was heard. A few moments later, a big pariah dog ran in through a gap in the fence. It bore the unmistakable appearance of a rabid animal, staring eyes, rough hair, staggering gait, frothing mouth. The foolish Tip, jealous of all canine intruders, at once made for the pariah, and in an instant two dogs were engaged in a fierce fight.

At that time the Pasteur Institute at Bangkok had just been opened, but Muang had certainly never heard of it. So far as he knew, the bite of a mad dog meant almost certain death of a most agonising kind. Yet he did not hesitate or waste any time, but sprang instantly upon the fighting dogs, seized one with each hand and dragged them apart. Then, thrusting Tip aside, he lifted up the mad dog by its neck, carried it struggling across the garden, and threw it down a disused well, where it was later shot. The foolish Tip emerged from this encounter with no apparent injury, but Muang had been severely bitten on the left forearm.

Luang Maitri was astonished by the great courage and determination shown by his friend the "pu-mia."

"Why did you do it?" he asked. "Did you not realize the danger? I would never have dared to seize that mad dog with my bare hands, as you did."

All that Muang had to say was:— "I could not let poor Tip be hurt." He did not seem to worry much about his injuries, but Luang Maitri explained to him the necessity of going at once to Bangkok for treatment. There was an express train due to leave in an hour's time.

"You must agree to be a man for a month," said the Assistant Judge. We do not want to waste time with useless explanations, or have any argument as to the proper ward into which you are to be put in the hospital. Leave it all to me. I have a brother who is a government doctor. I will wire to him, and he will meet you at the station and attend to the whole business."

*   *   *

139

So a suitcass was hurriedly packed with a few clothes and Muang, rigged out in one of Luang Maitri's suits, and looking very smart and alert as a young man, especially after his hair had been trimmed and the lipstick effect toned down, set out for the railway station.

"After all," said he, "I have only been a woman for two and a half years, and I can very well become a man again, if I choose to do so. No doubt half the girls in Bangkok will fall in love with me."

In this spirit he boarded the train, not at all nervous of the long journey to new and strange surroundings, nor of the unknown medical treatment awaiting him.

*   *   *

When Luang Maitri was next in Bangkok, he asked his brother, the doctor, what he thought of Nai Muang, and whether he had noticed anything unusual about him.

"I liked him immensely," said the doctor, "and so did the people at the Pasteur Institute. He is, or course, a very good-looking and well-set-up young fellow. Moreover, he is intelligent and has excellent manners. As you know, I am keen on boxing, and when his treatment was finished, I gave him several boxing lessons. He showed great promise, and has plenty of pluck. I observed nothing unusual about him, except that he used a good deal of perfume, and was rather fond of powdering his face. I was so pleased with him that I offered him a job down here as receptionist, but he told me he must return to Chiengmai, as he had an aged relative to look after."

So Muang went back to Chiengmai, and suffered no ill effects from the mad dog's bite. The morning after his return, he became a girl once more, and was to be seen, as before, seated at his loom, weaving a silk skirt.

"I am a man down South, but a woman up North," said he.

Life went on peacefully for several months. Luang Maitri continued to give lessons to Muang, teaching him, among other things, the rudiments of English. Muang, as before, helped with the Judge's laundry and cooking.

Then a change came over Muang's life. His old grandmother died, and he had more time to himself. He started to go about much more than before, and made a number of new friends. A cousin of his, a pretty girl from Lampang, came to stay with him and his mother, and often took his place at the loom.

It was the "Ok Wasa" Festival — the end of the Buddhist Lent. On the occasion of that festival a year before, Muang had brought Luang Maitri a present of an embroidered silk skirt, which he had woven himself. This year, to the Judge's astonishment, he brought him a beautifully made teak chair. with wicker seat.

After thanking Muang, Luang Maitri said:— "My dear young friend, it was truly kind of you to bring me this wonderful chair, but you really ought not to spend all that money on me."

To his surprise, Muang answered:— "It cost me nothing, Sir. I made it myself. I have struck up a friendship with Nai Wong the carpenter, and he has been giving me lessons in carpentry. He says I am getting on very well. I go there to help him every day, and from now on he intends to pay me a small salary. I do very little weaving now. My cousin has taken charge of all that work, and does it just as well as I can, better maybe. She is a very nice, hardworking girl, but she gets hold of foolish ideas at times. She has actually taken to locking her bedroom door at night, because she says her mother told her she should always do so when in a house with a young man! Did you ever hear anything so ridiculous in all your life?"

Luang Maitri looked well at Muang, and began to realize that a subtle change had begun to come over him. After all, this was the same young fellow who had boldly tackled a mad dog, and who had been readily accepted as a man in Bangkok — a man who showed promise as an amateur boxer. Was it really so very ridiculous for his pretty cousin to lock the door of her bedroom? When all was said and done, the Judge reflected, a skirt and a permanent wave cannot turn a man into a woman.

However, he let the matter pass without comment

Not long after this, Luang Maitri was called down to Bangkok on special duty, which kept him there for over two months. When he returned, the first person he saw on the railway platform was Muang — but not Muang the Pu-Mia. This was the smart, well-set-up young man who had returned from Bangkok the year before. The Judge could not conceal a look of surprise. Muang, seeing this, at once said:—

"Do not be surprised, Sir, to see me dressed as a man. I have given up being a Pu-Mia. Nai Wong the carpenter has taken me into partnership, and we are doing very well. He says I have doubled his business."

"My dear Muang," exclaimed Luang Maitri, "I am truly delighted to hear this. Man or woman, you will always be my good friend. With you turning out furniture and your cousin weaving skirts, you will soon be rich people. Or has she perhaps gone back to Lampang?"

"No, Sir," replied Muang, "she has not gone back, and she has no intention of going. She is going to marry me, and we were thinking of asking to borrow your car tomorrow, to drive to the District Office to register our marriage."

Luang Maitri was overjoyed. "This is great news!" he exclaimed. "Things could not possibly have turned out better. Next thing, you will be having a family."

"I am pretty sure we shall, Sir," answered Muang. "In fact, that is why we are in rather a hurry to get married. We would have done so before this, only we were very anxious to have you as one of our witnesses. You see, about the time when you left for Bangkok, my cousin lost the key of her bedroom!"

*   *   *

THE LOVE PHILTRE

Noi Chune was a great, tall, strong fellow, capable of doing almost any sort of hard work; but he had no brains.

When he was a tiny boy, his parents sent him to the village school at Nong Hoi, near Chiengmai, in Northern Thailand

There he learnt to read and write, and to do simple sums in arithemetic, but his teacher sent in the same report every term:— "Boy Chune is a very good pupil, well-behaved and polite, works hard and plays football well — but he has no brains."

When his parents decided that any attempt to drive more learning into his head would be a waste of money, Chune was ordained, at the age of sixteen, as a novice in Stone Pillar Temple. He remained there for four years, learnt how to chant a few Pali hymns, as well as the rudiments of Buddhist philosophy. The Head Priest thought well of him, and reported that he was an exemplary young man, always attending assiduously to his religious duties, willing and helpful in every way, — but not possessing any brains.

So Chune left the temple, bearing the honourable prefix of "Noi," a title conferred on ex-novices, and joined the army. He served for two years, winning golden opinions from his superiors for smartness and good conduct — but always with the qualification that he had no brains.

Noi Chune did not waste any time in worrying about his lack of brains. He went back home and took over charge of his elderly father's rice-fields and farm. He soon found that he was capable of raising a better rice crop than most of his neighbours, his cauliflowers were the biggest for miles around, and his pigs, geese and chickens always won half the prizes at the annual Chiengmai fair. So he felt pretty well able to carry on without brains. What troubled him was that he had lost his heart. He had lost it to his cousin, Kam Nuan.

Kam Nuan was a tiny little creature, two years younger than Noi Chune. She had never been of much use at any work requiring physical strength, and she was a rabbit at all games; but she was full of brains.

Even in the days of her infancy, all the neighbours agreed that she was far the brainiest child in the village. At school she was always at the top of her class, and her teachers reported that she had the most remarkable brains they had ever come across.

So when she had learnt everything the village school could teach, she was sent to the best secondary school in the neighbourhood. In three years there was nothing more they could teach her there, so off she went to Bangkok to study at the Chulalongkorn University. She returned at the age of twenty-one with a B.A. degree, and the reputation of being the most intelligent girl in Chiengmai. In almost no time, in spite of her youth, she was made Headmistress of one of the Government girls' schools.

Chune and Kam Nuan had been sweethearts in the days when they attended the village school together. But though he had never forgotten her, and had often thought of her when he was a novice in the temple (though he knew it was a sin to do so) she had been far too busy cultivating her own brain to have any time left over to dream about her childish romance.

Kam Nuan had not been very long back in Chiengmai when Chune sought her out, and said:—

"Little Sister, (for so he had always called her). I am only a stupid chap, with no brains, but I love you. I loved you when we were children together, and my heart has never changed. Now I am a man, and you are a woman. If you will marry me, I will be a true and loving husband to you until I die. I am not poor. My fields and garden yield good crops, I am doing a flourishing business in pigs and poultry, I have built myself a fine teak house, and I own a Jeep. I know I am unworthy of a clever girl like you, but I beg you to think over my offer before turning it down."

Kam Nuan shed a few tears, but she hardened her heart and said:—

"Big Brother, I have always loved you, and I love you still, but only as your Little Sister. We have followed different paths since we were childish sweethearts, and our lives have drifted apart. If I married you, maybe we would soon tire of one another. I would want to talk about all sorts of things which would only bore you — Shakespeare's plays, Browning's poems, Scott's novels, the movements of the planets, nuclear research, child welfare, the Communist threat, and a hundred other subjects, which you care nothing about. Then you would tell me about your crops and your pigs and your geese and your chickens, in which I am not much interested; and in the end we should come to irritate one another. You must marry a nice, sensible village girl, who has been brought up to be a

144

farmer's wife, and will be a real companion and help to you. And I will marry a doctor or a schoolmaster, who has the same sort of interests as myself. You will always be my Big Brother, and I your Little Sister. But better leave it so, and we shall both be happier."

Chune was not convinced by these specious arguments. However, he did not try to argue with so clever a girl as Kam Nuan, but went sadly home, and tried to overcome his disappointment by working harder than he had ever done before.

In a Thai village nothing remains secret for long. It very soon became known that Noi Chune the farmer had offered marriage to Miss Kam Nuan, the schoolmistress, and had been turned down, and it was plain to all that Noi Chune was feeling very unhappy.

A couple of weeks later, Chune received a visit from an aged woman named Yai Tip, who lived near by. This Yai Tip, without being exactly regarded as a witch, was looked upon with some awe by the village people. She was secretly consulted for charms to cure various sorts of sickness, for spells to get rid of evil spirits, or for other aid of an occult nature.

Adopting a mysterious and confidential manner, Yai Tip, after some rambling talk, came to the point, saying:— "Noi Chune, I know that you are feeling unhappy and distressed because the girl you love does not return your affection. But this is a very simple matter to set right. I have often been able to help other young men in a difficulty of this kind. For the very moderate fee of twenty Bahts I will prepare for you a magic philtre. If the girl you want to marry can be induced to swallow even the tiniest speck of this, her indifference will vanish, and she will love you as much as you can possibly desire."

"You wicked old woman" answered Chune with indignation "do you want me to get an innocent girl to swallow some horrible, poisonous drug which will make her ill, or perhaps even kill her?"

"Far from it," replied the old hag; "My philtre is perfectly harmless, and contains only pure and healthy ingredients.

145

It is the magic spell which I shall pronounce over it which will do the trick."

Noi Chune hesitated for a long time. However, as I think I have mentioned once or twice before, he had no brains, so in the end he yielded to the blandishments of the elderly enchantress, and agreed to purchase her magic philtre.

The procedure was a follows. Chune was to give Kam Nuan a small basket of lamut fruit. Yai Tip would prepare her magic philtre, into which she would dip a needle. Then she would pierce each lamut fruit with the needle — and all that Chune had then to do was to take the basket of fruit to Kam Nuan and await results.

The following morning Chune, still filled with doubt and apprehension took his basket of fruit to Kam Nuan's house, gave it to her, and returned home.

His nervousness increased from hour to hour. When evening came, he could bear the suspense no longer, so set off once more for Kam Nuan's house. When he got there, he was filled with terror and dismay to find her lying on a long chair, looking pale and distreessed. Seeing her in this condition, he at once concluded that his worst fears had been realized, that Yai Tip's magic philtre had poisoned her, and that she was no doubt on the point of death.

In an agony of remorse, he flung himself at Kam Nuan's feet and with tears in his eyes, blurted out the whole story.

"Little Sister," he cried, "I am the most miserable sinner and the biggest fool in the whole world. I love you more than anything on earth, yet I believed that wicked old woman, and so have caused you all this suffering. If you die, I will tie a stone round my neck and jump into the river."

At first Kam Nuan was filled with anger and indignation to think that Chune should have dared to play her such a trick, though she knew very well that her sicknes was not due to the fruit he had given her. She began to reproach him in bitter terms. Then, when she looked at the great, tall, strong fellow kneeling and weeping at her feet, her heart was softened towards him. She stopped talking, and thought to herself:—

"After all, he never *did* have any brains, but he loves me, and it was for love of me that he was persuaded to try this

146

idiotic trick. Who am I do despise him, anyhow? Can I plough or reap a field, to provide food for hundreds of people? Do I know how to breed animals and poultry for sale, or how to raise vegetables? What can I do but try to drive a lot of useless knowledge into the empty heads of a class of foolish children? He is the dear Big Brother of my childhood's days. Who else will look after me so well or love me so truly as he? If I marry him, maybe I can teach him a few things, and maybe, too, I shall find that I can learn a good deal from him."

Her angry frown changed to a smile, and she said:— "Big Brother, my sickness was not caused by the fruit you gave me. I was feeling rather unwell even before you brought it to me, so I ate none of it. You can see it, untouched, on the table over there. I am sure I shall be all right by tomorrow, so do not worry. And perhaps Yai Tip was not such a fraud as you think. Her love philtre may be worked after all. I held the fruit in my hand for a few moments. Maybe the magic philtre brought about a change in me. Who can tell? A few weeks ago you came here and asked me a question. The answer I gave disappointed and grieved you. If you feel inclined to ask me that same question again now, maybe I would give you a different answer."

Chune did not waste many seconds in taking her at her word. This time her answer was of a kind which sent him back home with such a broad smile on his face that old Yai Tip, who met him on the road, had no difficulty in guessing how things had turned out.

"Young Master," she croaked, "I can see that my philtre has worked. How about giving me a bit extra for making such a quick job of it?"

"You wicked old wretch," exclaimed Chune, "your charm was a fraud. She never ate any of the fruit at all!"

"How can you call me a fraud?" asked the old woman. "My philtre worked all right. Anyone can see that with half an eye, by merely looking at the smile on your face!"

Chune was feeling so happy that he got out a twenty Baht note, and held it up, saying:— "All right, Grandma, I will give you this for a present. But first you have got to tell me the real truth. What was your magic philtre made of?"

"Coconut milk — just pure coconut milk," chuckled the old crone. "As I told you, it was prefectly harmless. But it worked all the same, didn't it?"

So Big Brother and Little Sister got married after all, and are as happy as any man and woman have the right to be. She tells him all about Shakespeare's plays, Browning's poems, Scott's novels, the movements of the planets, nuclear research, child welfare, the Communist threat, and a hundred other subjects, and he laps it all up and asks for more. And he tells her all about his rice and cauliflower crops and the family history of his geese and chickens and his pigs, and she listens entranced, and can never have enough of it. And when they have exhausted their own particular subjects, they still have another inexhaustible topic for discussion — their twin babies, a boy and a girl, now a year old The boy is exactly like his mother, and the girl is the living image of her father, and both of them are chock-full of brains — or so their parents say. And who am I to doubt their word?

*   *   *

GOLDEN EYE

His eye — he had only one — was not really golden; it was a sort of tawny yellow, but his owner, Chao Inta of Wieng Wai, in Northern Siam, thought it a beautiful eye; so *Golden Eye* became his official name. He was a camel; not a beautiful, glossy, active young camel, but an aged and rather mangy creature.

Chao Inta considered himself to be a zoologist He had in his garden a number of cages, containing various wild beasts; a scabby lion, a scrofulous tiger, a smelly bear — not to mention a tank containing an evil-looking crocodile. When, therefore, during a visit to Bangkok, he came across a real live camel, it was only natural that he should offer to buy it. Its owner, the proprietor of a travelling menagerie, was easily persuaded to sell his camel for four or five times the amount

148

he had paid for it. Thus it came about that this denizen of the sandy deserts was to be seen in the green, lush city of Wieng Wai, installed as the most important member of Chao Inta's zoo.

At first all the people of Wieng Wai were delighted with their Chief's wonderful camel. It soon became known that a hair from the tail of *Golden Eye,* burnt, powered, and swallowed in a glass of the local spirit, was a cure for every disease. Crowds followed him whenever he was taken for a walk round the city, and it soon became necessary to provide a special guard to protect the poor creature's tail against marauders.

The fame of *Golden Eye* soon spread throughout the whole of Northern Siam, and all the other Chiefs in that region were filled with envy. Some of them even contemplated the possibility of offering to marry Chao Inta's daughter, who was the most unattractive Princess in the whole of the North, in the hope of being able to acquire *Golden Eye* as part of her dowry.

It was early in the year 1872 when *Golden Eye* first made his appearance in Wieng Wai. Throughout the early months of that year he continued to be the idol and palladium of all the people of that State. As for Chao Inta, he looked upon *Golden Eye* as his most marvellous possession, and would not have been willing to dispose of him on any terms — not even to get rid of his daughter.

During the months of March and April, when the country was dry, hot and dusty, *Golden Eye* seemed full of life. A few thunderstorms occurred in April, and *Golden Eye* became fretful and ill-tempered; but when the month of May arrived, and the regular rains were due to begin, there was not a single cloud to be seen in the sky, and the old camel cheered up and became almost frisky. Then came June; still no rain. July, when ploughing should have been well under way, still dry and cloudless, and *Golden Eye* becoming daily more and more cheerful. The people began to grow anxious, and when mid-August was reached, and ploughing was still impossible, the farmers started to talk about famine.

A state of panic seemed to be approaching. Prayers for rain were held in every temple; enormous rockets were

149

shot up into the cloudless sky; a cat and a monkey were taken in solemn procession round the city, and ceremoniously dipped in the river. But it was all in vain. Neither the prayers, nor the rockets, nor the monkey, nor the cat had the slightest effect. The sky remained clear and cloudless, and the earth hard and dry.

Then at last old Pu Suk, who was looked upon as the wisest weather prophet and expert in the State, lifted up his voice and spoke. At a meeting held in the principal temple, he made this announcement:—

"The Chief's camel, *Golden Eye,* is the sole cause of all our troubles. He comes from a hot and dry land, where only a few drops of rain fall each year. He hates the rain which is as our very life to us, and by his magic power he has dried up the fountains of heaven. So long as he lives, we shall be in danger of famine and death."

It was instantly clear to the whole city that Pu Suk had spoken the truth. In previous years, when there was no camel in their midst, rain always fell in June. This year, owing to the baleful presence of *Golden Eye,* they were nearing the end of August without a drop of rain. The whole matter was clear and obvious, and so was the conclusion to be drawn from it. *Golden Eye* must die!

But who would dare to suggest to the Chief that his beloved camel should be killed? Any man making such a suggestion was certain to be soundly flogged, or worse. And any man daring to act as executioner on his own initiative would without doubt pay for such a crime with his own life. What was to be done?

Only one man found an answer to this question.

Phra Tabin was a novice in the temple of Dawning Glory. He was a young fellow of twenty, strong and vigorous, whose quick intelligence caused him to be looked upon as their leader by his eleven young fellow-novices. Late that night, he secretly called his companions together, and addressed them as follows:—

"My dear brethren and fellow-novices. You have all heard today of the pronouncement made by Pu Suk, that the Chief's camel, *Golden Eye,* is the cause of the terrible drought which is afflicting our State. Unless this is brought to an end at once, famine will be upon us, and thousands of people, old and young alike, will die. We are Buddhist novices, and are bound by a solemn oath to slay no sentient being; but we are faced with a choice; we must decide between the life of one animal and the lives of many human beings. I propose to cast lots, and the one among us who draws the fatal lot must kill the camel. Any man who disagrees, hold up his hand."

Nobody held up his hand, the lots were drawn, and to Tabin himself fell the task of saving the State from famine, even at the risk of committing a deadly sin.

At the dawn of day, Tabin sought out the Lord Abbot, and to him he divulged all that had passed. The Abbot, who was a deeply religious man, and had never in his life willingly killed any living creature, had a long struggle with his conscience. At last he said:—

"My son, I cannot blame you for the decision you have made. This is a special case, not covered by any ordinary rules. You must kill *Golden Eye*. But you must not perform this terrible deed while wearing the yellow robe. I must first dismiss you from the holy brotherhood, and absolve you from the vows you have taken."

Half an hour later, Tabin left the temple, wearing the clothes of an ordinary farmer, and with a palm-leaf hat on his head, and returned to his father's house. Before his ordination, he had been a keen hunter, and possessed a flint-lock gun, which he had put away in a box in his room. He got out this old weapon, loaded it, and took up a position behind the fence of his father's compound.

It was usual for the keeper of *Golden Eye* to take the camel out for exercise at about eight o'clock each morning, and they always passed in front of the house of Tabin's father. As a rule, there were not many people about at that hour, but on that fateful morning large crowds had assembled, and the street was lined with angry citizens yelling curses and objurgations at the poor old beast as it shuffled along.

As soon as the sound of the shouting came nearer, Tabin went close to the gate of the compound, and when the camel, followed by a raging throng, arrived opposite the gate, he rushed out before anyone had time to realise what was happening, put the barrel of his gun close against the head of *Golden*

Eye, and fired. The camel fell down in the road and died almost at once.

It is impossible to describe the consternation of the crowd. Excitement, fear and joy were all mingled. The babel was astounding. In the midst of all this ferment, Tabin was seized by the Chief's adherents who accompanied the unhappy victim, and borne away to the palace.

The rage of Chao Inta knew no bounds; he gave immediate orders that Tabin was to receive a hundred strokes with a rattan, and that at three o'clock that same afternoon he was to be publicly beheaded in the market square. His son, Chao Mano, who secretly shared the general opinion that *Golden Eye* was responsible for the drought, ventured to intercede for the culprit.

"Look at the sky, Father," said he; "There are a few dark clouds gathering on the horizon. Maybe there is some truth in what the people have been saying. Wait till tomorrow before you have Tabin executed."

The Chief struck his son in the face. "How dare you plead for the scoundrel who has murdered my beloved *Golden Eye*," he shouted. "The fellow is an ordained novice, yet has committed this frightful murder. He is a wretch outside the pale of humanity."

Then to his attendants he said:— "Lock up Chao Mano along with his friend the murderer until I have decided how to punish him. I will teach him to respect his father and his Chief."

Tabin duly received the hundred strokes, and was carried back, faint and bleeding, to await his execution.

* * *

At three that same afternoon, Tabin, half unconscious, was dragged out to the market square. There a platform had been erected, on which was a short teak post. To this post Tabin was tied, and made to kneel down. The executioner stood ready, sword in hand. He was not masked, as was formerly the custom in Western countries. Everybody knew him. He was a tough, hardened old wretch who had taken off quite a number of heads at the Chief's behest. But today he was afraid. A huge crowd of citizens had gathered in the square.

152

They were in an angry mood, shouting at the headsman, daring him to touch Tabin, and uttering threats even against the Chief himself.

During all this time, the black clouds earlier seen on the horizon had begun to spread across the sky. It was growing dark, and thunder could be heard both to the East and the West.

The Chief, furious, strode to the side of the platform. "Do your duty, executioner!" he shouted, "what are you waiting for?"

The executioner looked at the Chief's threatening face. Then he looked at the crowd, and saw five thousand threatening faces. He flung his sword to the ground. "I will not execute this man," he cried. "He has done no wrong. He has saved us all from famine. Look! Look! Here it comes! Rain! Rain!!"

As he uttered these words, the whole sky seemed to burst open. Rain, rain, rain! Torrents, oceans of rain! Never had such rain been seen within living memory. In a few minutes the whole square, the whole city, the whole country-side were inches deep in water. And still it rained.

A mighty shout of relief and thankfulness went up from the crowd. They stormed the platform, they released Tabin, they seized the Chief and called on the executioner to cut off his head. But the crowd was so dense and the confusion so great that Chao Inta fell to the earth and was trampled underfoot before anyone knew what was happening. Then a voice in the crowd called out:— "Chao Inta is dead; bring forth Chao Mano and we will make him our Chief in his father's place; for he tried to defend our dear brother Tabin, who has saved us all from famine by slaying that evil camel."

All day and all the next night it rained, and next morning every field was covered with water, and every farmer was busy with his plough, and every ox and buffalo hard at work. And the crop that year, though late, was the best that had been seen for generations.

Chao Mano became Chief, and ruled his people wisely and justly, not tyrannically, as his father, the owner and patron of *Golden Eye,* had done.

As for Tabin, he could have claimed, and received, any reward he fancied. He was a national hero and idol. But all he said was:— "I committed a sin in slaying the camel, though I did so with good intentions. Still, I must go back to the temple and be re-ordained as a novice. Thus only can I expiate my sin. Next year I will become a fully ordained monk."

And so he did. And when he died, still a monk, seventy years later, he was regarded on all sides as a saint; but few remembered how he had killed *Golden Eye,* the camel, for memories are short in Northern Siam.

*   *   *

GINGER

John Clare, known to his friends as "Ginger," was a young Englishman employed by the Thai Government in their Forest Department. As a keen collector of rare orchids, he found his job, which took him often into the deepest recesses of the jungle, very congenial. On the morning of the day on which this story opens, Ginger had left his tent at the foot of Doi Ku Mountain in Nan Province, and had climbed some distance up the mountain to visit a small settlement of Yao hill tribesmen, having been told by some of his servants that these Yaos were in the habit of cultivating various kinds of little-known orchids, which their women-folk used to decorate their hair on festive occasions.

It was a very tiny settlement, and when Ginger got there he found only two people in the village, an old man and a young woman. The woman appeared to be about twenty-five years of age — the same age as himself. She was pretty, with the pink-and-white complexion and light brown hair so often seen among the Yaos, and was wearing a spray of rare orchids in her hair. He asked her if she had any orchids to sell. She appeared to understand, and was able to speak a few words of Thai.

"Come this way," she said, and led him towards one of the huts which made up the village. When they reached the door, she said something to the old man; he immediately turned and went away in the direction of the forest. The girl then entered the hut, and Ginger followed her.

There were several baskets of orchids hanging up in the hut. The girl took two of these down and handed them to Ginger. When he asked her how much she wanted for them, she shook her head and said, "I give you." This seemed very unusual, and the glance with which she accompanied her words was equally unexpected. Ginger had not reached the age of twenty-five without having discovered that he was not altogether without attraction to some members of the opposite sex, but he found it hard to believe that he could have aroused any amorous feelings in the heart of this daughter of a forest tribe, whom he had only met a few minutes before. Then he remembered reading in a book he had recently come across a statement to the effect that the Yaos and Meows were distinctly lax and easy-going in regard to sexual matters, sharply contrasting in this respect with the Karen and Lu tribes.

"Better not encourage her," he thought. "The old man or some of the villagers may be back any moment, and they might not like to find me here with her. I'll clear out."

He picked up the orchids, said "Thank you — and good-bye," and stretched out his hand in a farewell gesture. The girl seized his hand, kissed it, or rather sniffed at it, and started to stroke his arm. Ginger, though no Casanova, was not entirely without experience, and he realised at once what she wanted. Indeed, even a Trappist monk could hardly have been mistaken.

However, Ginger was a pretty level-headed fellow, not easily a prey to desire or emotion. He turned away and left the hut. The girl followed him weeping, less it seemed in sorrow than in anger. Ginger remembered the words:—
"Hell knows no fury like a woman scorned."

After walking a couple of hundred yards from the village, Ginger sat down on a fallen tree-trunk to take breath and pull himself together. The experience he had just been through was something quite unexpected, and had taken him completely by surprise. Now he tried to think the matter over

155

in the cold light of reason. His thoughts were something like this:—

"Curious that this young woman should have taken such a fancy to me. I wonder if she behaves like that with every strange young man who visits the village! I have heard stories of young Thai men being forcibly compelled to become the lovers of hill tribes-women. A jolly good thing I cleared out! Still, I wonder if she thought me a sanctimonious ass. After all, I was not nearly so easily scared by that girl at Blackpool, or that French girl on board ship. Am I really growing to be a bit of prig? After all, I would have committed myself to nothing if I had stayed. And the girl really is rather pretty, and not nearly so dirty-looking as the hill people usually are. Still, I was very wise not to stay. I am sure I was right. I will go straight down to my camp at the foot of the mountain and forget about the whole business."

Then he stood up, hesitated for a few moments, and walked back to the village.

*　　　*　　　*

Three years passed by. In that space of time many changes had taken place in the life of Ginger Clare. A few weeks after his adventure on the Doi Ku mountain he had gone home to England on furlough. On the journey home he had fallen in with one of the directors of the Anglo-Holland Petroleum Company. A friendship had sprung up between the two men, and Ginger had been offered a post as Chiengmai Manager of the Company's business. So he sent in his resignation to the Forest Department, and had returned to Chiengmai as a business man. And not only as a business man, but also as a Benedick.

During his short stay in England, Ginger had fallen in love with Evelyn Dacre, the daughter of the vicar of his native village in Somerset. Having now a steady and well-paid occupation, nothing stood in the way of his marriage. So, after a lightning courtship, a quiet village wedding, and a honeymoon spent on board ship, we find Ginger and Evelyn installed in an idyllic bungalow on the banks of the River Me Ping at Chiengmai.

156

After two years of married life, Ginger and Evelyn were more deeply in love with one another than at the time of their wedding. To Ginger, Evelyn was the perfect woman, and to Evelyn Ginger appeared as an almost faultless hero.

Only one cloud had arisen to darken their sky. They had both intended to raise a family of young Gingers, but, alas, something had gone wrong. A few months before their first child was due, Evelyn had fallen dawnstairs. An operation was found necessary. Evelyn recovered quickly, but she was given to understand that there was no hope of any more children.

This was a serious blow to Ginger and Evelyn. However, they made the best of it, and as time went by, they came to accept the inevitable without repining.

Then, one day, an elderly American Baptist missionary, the Reverend Mr. James Downing, and his wife, who had been stationed for several years at Nan and had recently been transferred to Chiengmai, came to call on Evelyn and Ginger. Evelyn happened to be out shopping. In the course of conversation, Mr. Downing said:— "A few months ago I ran up against a rather unusual occurrence. I was trying to do some work among the hill tribes north of Nan, and one day I paid a visit to a small Yao village on the Doi Ku mountain. The first thing I saw there, running along the village street, was a little boy about two years of age. He was, in appearance, pure European, with bright ginger hair and blue eyes. Of course, the Yaos are rather a fair-skinned tribe, but this little boy was far fairer than any of their children whom I had previously come across. I made enquiries concerning him, and was told the following story by an old man of the village, who professed to know all about it. Some three years earlier, a young foreigner, with ginger hair and blue eyes, had visited the village to buy orchids. A young woman of the village, whose husband had recently died, had taken a fancy to the stranger, and had induced him to stay with her for about an hour in her hut. Nine months later, this young woman had given birth to the little boy whom I had just seen. Not long after his birth, she had been accidentally killed by a falling tree in the forest. The old man, who was a relation of the child's mother, had taken charge of him and brought him up."

"My wife and I are old. We had only one child — a son, who died recently. He was married, but had no children We had always hoped to have grandchildren. I felt sure that my wife would be delighted by the little ginger-haired boy, so I offered to buy him from the old Yao. Maybe he was glad to get rid of him. Anyhow, he sold him to me for two hundred bahts. When I got home, my wife was charmed with the little boy, and he is here in Chiengmai with us now. We intend to bring him up as our own child.

"We have often wondered who can have been the father of this child. His birth would seem to have been the result of a very chance encounter. But be that as it may, we feel that perhaps God has sent him to us to be a comfort in our old age."

Ginger was deeply disturbed by this story. Long before Mr. Downing had finished speaking, he realised the truth. That day, three years ago, when after a rather half-hearted struggle with his conscience, he had returned to the Yao village, he had imagined that it was only a question of a little transitory pleasure — a question of "Gather ye rosebuds while ye may." Now he saw that this was not so. That chance encounter had resulted in the birth of a human being, a little boy with ginger hair and blue eyes, just like himself. He stood up and said to Mr. Downing:

"Look at me, Sir! Look at me well. I am a tall man I have ginger hair and blue eyes. Three years ago I visited a Yao village on the Doi Ku mountain. There I spent an hour alone in a hut with a young Yao woman. God forgive me! The child is mine!"

Mr. and Mrs. Downing took a long look at Ginger. There was no possible doubt about it. The little boy they had adopted was his son. Even if he had not admitted it, they would have known it to be so.

Then Ginger went on. "This will be a terrible blow to my wife; but I must tell her. She has been very strictly brought up, and the thought that I have had a child with a jungle woman whom I never saw before will shock her beyond words. You, dear Mrs. Downing, have seen a lot of the world and perhaps you can understand how a young man may sometimes yield to a sudden temptation. What happened that day on the mountain was just like the meeting and mating of two wild animals of the forest, without thought and without meaning.

"I will not excuse myself or try to explain my conduct. Still, I beg you not to think too harshly of me. Though this little boy has come into the world unwanted and unexpected, I am ready to do my duty by him. I cannot, I fear, bring him up myself; to that my wife would never agree. But if, in the goodness of your hearts, you will continue to take care of him, I must take my full share of the expense of his upbringing and education.

"Above all, I want to see my son. Please go back to your house and bring him here. My wife will be back any minute, and I will confess everything to her. It has got to be done some time. Better get it over, come what may."

Mr. and Mrs. Downing agreed, and set forth for their home to bring the little boy. Hardly had they departed when Evelyn returned. Ginger wasted no time. He related the whole story to his wife, concealing nothing, excusing nothing.

Evelyn took this disclosure more philosophically than Ginger had feared she would do. She wept a little, then she laughed a little. Then she wept again. "Perhaps I was a fool," she said, "to imagine that you were any different from other men. After all, I can read, and anyone who can read in these days cannot help knowing a good deal about the faults and follies of young people of both sexes. I have had girl friends who behaved just as badly as you did. I will do my best to forget about the whole thing. But I must ask you never to bring the little boy here. I could not bear to see him. The sight of him would remind me of my own loss, and my soul would rebel against God. I would never cease to question His justice for giving to a wild forest woman the blessing which He denied to me. And I would hate the poor child, who has done me no wrong. He must stay with Mr. and Mrs. Downing."

She had hardly finished speaking when the voices of Mr. and Mrs. Downing were heard. Evelyn looked out of the window, and saw them coming in along the garden path; and

Mrs. Downing was carrying in her arms — little Ginger. There was no mistaking him. He was a complete replica in miniature of her husband — anyone would have picked them out as father and son had they been in a crowd of a thousand people.

A few seconds later, and the old missionaries were in the room. Mrs. Downing put down the little boy, and he started to toddle about the floor. When she looked at him, Evelyn felt her heart soften towards him, and she said to herself:

"Maybe this is God's way of comforting me for the loss of my own unborn child. Who am I to question His justice and His wisdom? I had hoped and prayed for a little Ginger, looking just like my own dear Ginger. And here he is, raised by a miracle out of the forest."

Then she knelt down, and took the little child in her arms.

Mr. Downing whispered to his wife:— "He belongs here. We cannot keep him. He has found his real father, and a new mother."

Then the old people crept silently away from the room, and Evelyn was left alone with her two Gingers — father and son.

THE RETURN

A young farmer of Northern Thailand stood in front of his tiny bamboo house and called to his grandmother within.

"Granny, please have my supper ready in about an hour. I am going to the temple."

"You have been working at the plough all day, Noi," answered the old woman. "Stay at home and rest a while before your supper. Ever since that worthless hussy went away and left you, you have spent all your evenings in the temple. Religion is all very well, but one can have too much of it."

"Do not worry me, Granny. My heart is ill at ease. Only when I am kneeling before the image of the Holy One do I find a little peace and forgetfulness."

It was just over a month since Noi's pretty girl-wife, Bua Kham, had gone off with a rich Chinese trader from Bangkok. At first his only feelings had been those of rage and jealousy, but now he was beginning fo find excuses for her.

"I am so poor," he thought, "so miserably poor, and she is so beautiful. What had I to offer her? With that rich Chinese, even though she will only be his number two wife, she will want for nothing. Why should she work as a mere drudge in my little bamboo hut?"

With thoughts such as these, Noi made his way across the rice-field towards the village temple. When he was about to enter the temple gate, he felt a light touch on his arm. Turning, he saw Bua Kham.

"Husband," she whispered, "I have come back. Do not drive me away. I was mad — mad. We were so poor, and that horrible old Chinaman tempted me. He gave me what looked like a pair of diamond ear-rings, and he promised to buy me a motor-car if I would follow him to Bangkok. And when I got there, my life was like hell. His head wife treated me as a slave. She took away my ear-rings, allowed me no money, and hardly gave me enough food to eat. As for that evil old man, he soon lost all interest in me. He had two other women there beside his head wife. They all despised me because I am an ignorant Northern girl and cannot read or write. When I wept or complained, the head wife threatened to sell me to a brothel."

"I would have run away within a week, but I had no money. A few days ago, I found out where my ear-rings were hidden. As soon as I had an opportunity I took them away and pawned them. And after all they proved to be worth very little. I only got just enough money to pay my third class train fare. I had no food to eat during the twenty hour railway journey, except a few small cakes given me by a kind-hearted old lady on the train. I have had to come on foot all the thirty miles from the station. I am tired and hungry. Forgive me, husband. I have had my lesson. Pity me and forgive me."

"I cannot answer you yet," replied Noi. "Come into the temple with me. We will kneel together before the image of the Lord Buddha, and I will seek His guidance."

Noi had brought with him four joss-sticks. Two of these he gave to Bua Kham. Then, side by side, they entered the dark temple, lit their joss-sticks, and knelt in supplication before the great image.

For a long time Noi prayed. Then he raised his eyes and looked at the calm face of the golden Buddha. The Holy One's eyes seemed to gaze back at him, and a soundless voice to say:—

"Foolish young man, why do you let your soul be troubled by the changes and losses of this transient life? Human existence is nothing but a ceaseless succession of changes. As soon as you were born, you began to die. Your wife left you; she has returned; she may leave you again and return again. What does it all matter? Such things are but links in the endless succession of changes which make up man's existence. I alone never change. As I was yesterday, so I am today, and so shall I be tomorrow and for endless ages to come. Put your trust in me and follow my law, and you will come to see how meaningless and trivial are all the fleeting joys and sorrows of human life."

And Noi answered in his heart:— "O Holy One, Thou hast shown me the right path. I will follow it in faith and hope."

Then he arose, and gently touched Bua Kham on the shoulder.

"Come, wife," he said, "let us go home. My grandmother will have supper waiting. There will be enough for the two of us tonight. Tomorrow I must get up early to follow the plough, and you must cook my mid-day meal and bring it to me in the rice-field. We will eat it together in the shade of the big flame-of-the-forest tree."

HEROIN

"Your wife is a heroin addict, Corporal Viros," said the doctor. "She has been taking the drug in large quantities for some months past. This is the reason for her having a miscarriage after only four months pregnancy. I am sorry to tell you that the child will be born dead. As for your wife, the only hope for her is for you to leave her with us in the hospital. We will put her through a course of treatment which may eradicate the habit. But we cannot make any definite promise. Some cases are incurable."

Corporal Viros Sripanya, of the Wieng Wai Police Force, was thunderstruck by this disclosure. For a long time past he had noticed a subtle change in his wife, Lamduan. She had grown very thin, and alternated between listlessness and bursts of excitement about nothing in particular. Whenever he had suggested that she should consult a doctor, she had angrily refused to do so.

They had been married for less than a year. He had first noticed a change in her only a few months after their marriage, but it was not very evident, and when, later on, her symptoms became more marked, he had put it down to her pregnancy.

Finally, she had suddenly been seized by the pains of premature labour, and he had hurried her to the hospital. Now came this shattering announcement that she was a heroin addict, and that the longed-for baby was to be born dead.

A dreary prospect lay before Viros. He loved his wife dearly, and never thought of abandoning her now that she had become a drug addict. On the other hand, he was a poor man, and hardly knew where he would be able to find enough money to keep her in the hospital until she was cured. But on one point his mind was quickly made up. He would find out from Lamduan the name of the man or woman who had initiated her into the heroin habit, and had supplied her with the drug, and would see to it that the culprit was brought to justice.

As soon as Lamduan had recovered a little after her troublesome labour, he pressed her to tell him the name of

163

the person who had lured her into the drug habit; but she steadily refused to tell him. "I am afraid," said she; "the people who trade in heroin belong to a big organisation, and have agents all over the place. If I were to get one of their agents into trouble, my life would not be safe. Moreover, I would be unable to obtain any more heroin, and then I would die."

But it soon became apparent that she would die in any case. Her constitution was naturally delicate, and had been so undermined by the use of heroin that she was unable to withstand the strain of her premature confinement. She gradually became weaker and weaker, until at last Viros was warned that she had only a few more days to live.

Then, at last, she told him the whole truth. One day, not long after their marriage, a man had called at their house, after Viros had gone to work, offering medicines for sale. She was suffering at the time from a bad cold. The pedlar had sold her a bottle of medicine for a very small sum. This had not only relieved her cold, but had produced in her a feeling of well-being and exhilaration. When the man called again, she bought two more bottles, and later on several more. By this time she found that she was unable to do without the medicine, and the pedlar told her frankly that it was mainly composed of heroin, and that she would have to go on taking it. Moreover, he raised the price. But she was helpless. She had to go on taking the drug, and she had to pay any price which was demanded for it. She took to going without her midday meal, and used the money thus saved to pay for the drug. Moreover, she secretly sold most of the jewellery which her parents had given her at the time of her marriage. In addition, she had borrowed various sums of money from their neighbours.

Now she was dying, and had no longer any reason to fear the vengeance of the dope-dealers. The man who had lured her on to become an addict, and who had sold her the heroin, she said, was a Chinese named Lee Sae Kuang, and he lived some miles away from the city, across the padi fields, at a small village called Ban Saek. There he and his friends prepared the heroin, and from thence they distributed it to their victims.

As soon as Lamduan was dead, Viros made up his mind to prepare a report on the whole matter and submit it to the Police Major in charge of his station, and to file it the next morning. He sat up half the night preparing his report.

On his arrival at the Police Station the next morning, and before he had time to present his report, his Sergeant addressed him as follows:—

"Late last night we received information to the effect that one Lee Sae Kuang, a Chinese, is carrying on a trade in heroin at a village called Ban Saek, across the padi fields along the Chiengrak road. Take the station jeep and drive at once to the nearest point on the road, then cross the fields and search this man's premises. If you find any heroin or any apparatus for preparing it, arrest Lee or any other suspicious characters, bring them across the fields to the jeep, and drive them straight back here. I am sorry I can only send one man with you, Private Sakdi, as a number of our men have just been sent out to investigate a murder case."

Viros thought to himself:— "I will hold up my report, and will go and see this scoundrel for myself first."

Everything went as planned. Corporal Viros and Private Sakdi were driven a couple of miles along the Chiengrak road, then they left the jeep in charge of the driver, and started to walk across the fields. When nearing the village of Ban Saek, they met one of the inhabitants, and obtained from him exact details as to the position of Lee's house. Thus they were able to swoop down upon their suspect without any chance of his being warned beforehand. As it happened, Lee was alone in the house when they entered it. They at once handcuffed him, and then made a thorough search of the house. There they found abundant evidence against Lee; quantities of heroin, and a complete outfit for the preparation of the drug. They seized the whole outfit, and put it in charge of the village kamnan. Then they set forth, with their prisoner, across the fields.

Lee was not unduly depressed at finding himself a prisoner. "Of course I shall plead guilty to all the charges that may be brought against me," said he: "then I shall get a light sentence."

But Viros thought to himself:— "Yes, he will plead guilty and get off with a light sentence. He has ruined my life, broken up my home, killed my wife and my unborn child, and plunged me into endless debt. Now, for a short space of time, he is in my power. Am I to take him back to plead guilty and get a nice, short term of imprisonment, and then come out to bring ruin and misery and death into some other happy household? Not if I can prevent it!"

Soon they came to a cluster of tree in the centre of the field. Viros pulled down his sleeve so as to conceal his wrist-watch. Then he said to Sakdi:— "I have lost my watch. The buckle of the strap was loose, and it must have fallen off in Lee's house. Please go back and bring it. It will only take you a few minutes. I will wait here under the trees and look after the prisoner. I shall be all right. My rifle is loaded."

Sakdi turned and walked quickly towards the village.

"Now or never!" thought Viros. "I have about five or six minutes to do the job!"

Then, turning to Lee, he said:— "Quick, before the policeman comes back. How much will you give me to let you escape?"

"Five thousand bahts," replied the Chinese.

"Done with you! I will get leave next Tuesday and go by train to Pitssnulok. Meet me at the Sri Prasert Hotel there. Now, hit me as hard as you can with your handcuffed hands, full in the face. Then run away as fast as your legs will carry you."

Lee struck him in the face with his full strength, then turned and ran. Before he had reached the edge of the open field, Viros shot him twice, once in the back, and once in the head.

"Pray Heaven that he will not live long enough to talk," thought Viros. "I deserve a bit of luck."

His luck held. Lee never spoke again. He was dead.

Less than a minute later, Sakdi, alarmed by the sound of shooting, came running full speed to the clump of trees. Lee lay dead, and Viros, with a bleeding forehead and a rapidly blackening left eye, stood, rifle in hand, about twenty yards away.

"He took me completely by surprise," explained Viros. "He suddenly struck me full in the face with his two hand-cuffed fists. The handcuffs cut my forehead, and I am sure

166

Lee struck him in the face with his full strength.

he has blackened my eye. Then, before I fully realised what had happened, I saw him running away towards the field. What else could I do but shoot at him? But I am sorry he is dead, because we shall not be able to get from him the names of his accomplices."

"That is certainly a pity," replied Sakdi. "Still I do not see how you could have acted otherwise. Nobody can possibly blame you. We had better carry him back to the jeep. And, by the way, I could not find your watch."

"Oh, my watch," said Viros off-handedly. "I had it in my pocket all the time, and had forgotten about it."

*   *   *

The kamnan was able to put the police onto the track of Lee's accomplices, and they were all arrested and sent to jail. As for the death of Lee, it was agreed on all hands that Viros was in no way to blame. In fact, he became almost a hero among his comrades. And not long afterwards, he was promoted to the rank of Sergeant. As for his written report, he tore it up. It seemed to him to be out of date.

Nobody but you and I, my dear reader, know what really happened. Do you blame Viros? I do not. I think he deserved his promotion, and I shall watch his future career with deep sympathy and interest. He deserved a bit of luck.

*   *   *

COCONUT MONKEY

His name was Bujang, which is Malay for a bachelor. I do not know whether he was really a bachelor, but it would have been difficult for him to have married, as he was always kept tied up. He was a coconut monkey — the hard-working slave of a human master.

Bujang was born and brought up in Kelantan, the State which, as all the world knows, produces the cleverest coconut monkeys. Both his parents were professional coconut monkeys, and he was only a few weeks old when his training began. He was made to wear a belt, to which a long rope was attached. Then he was taught to climb a coconut tree, and sit among a clump of nuts. He touched a nut. No answering tug from the trainer below. He touched another — and so on until an answering jerk of the rope told him to go ahead. Then he had to twist the stem of the coconut he had touched last, and keep on twisting until it fell to the ground. He learnt quickly, for coconut picking was in his blood, an art inherited from a long line of ancestors, maybe back to the days when Alexander the Great visited Malaya.

When Bujang was a year old, he was sold to Lung Plien, a Thai coconut planter of Patani. He soon learnt to understand Thai, and became known as the most skilful coconut monkey in the whole State of Patani. But though he worked hard and well, Lung Plien, who was a miserly old curmudgeon, did not care for him. He did not regard Bujang as a sentient and intelligent creature, but as a mere machine for bringing down coconuts. If ever poor Bujang made a mistake, by sending down the wrong coconut, or if he hesitated before getting to work, he was certain to be soundly beaten, or to have his long ears and his short tail sharply pulled.

Lung Plien was a widower, living in a small hut with only two companions — little Bujang, and a nephew aged twelve, named Boon Ma. Boon Ma was not much better treated than Bujang. He, too, was made to climb the coconut trees, and he, too, was often cruelly punished if his uncle was dissatisfied with his work. The boy and the monkey, companions in misfortune, soon became warmly attached to one another. When Boon Ma had any money, which was not often the case, he would spend it on nuts and bananas for Bujang, and at night they shared the same bed and the same blanket.

Boon Ma was an orphan. When his parents were still living, he had attended the village school, and had learnt to read and write. He was very anxious to continue his education, but when his parents died, and he was brought to live with his uncle, all such ambitions were firmly opposed. He was needed to help in the hut, and to work in the coconut garden. At night, he would often talk to Bujang, whispering into his ears the story of all his troubles. One night, after the boy

169

and the monkey had both been severely beaten, Boon Ma whispered:— "Little brother, how happy we both would be if only my uncle were to die. I would go to school and grow up to be a clever man, and you would have bananas and cakes to eat every day."

The next day, Bujang was sent up a coconut tree as usual. But on this occasion, a curious accident occurred. When Lung Plien indicated by the customary jerk of the rope that a particular nut was to be dropped down, the monkey twisted the stem correctly, but when the nut fell, instead of dropping vertically from the tree, it seemed to spring away in an outward direction, and struck Lung Plien on the shoulder. The old man was furiously angry. "That horrible little beast did that on purpose!" he yelled. "It wants to kill me. I will beat it to death."

Boon Ma was afraid that his uncle would really kill Bujang. "Do not blame the monkey," he pleaded, "it is too small and weak to be able to push away a large coconut so as to make it fall so far from the tree." At the same time a neighbour, Pu Tan, happened to come into the garden; he, too, when he was told what had happened, was emphatic in maintaining that it was impossible for a small monkey to have influenced the direction in which the coconut was to fall.

Lung Plien was not much hurt by the coconut striking his shoulder, so he soon calmed down. Nevertheless, when Bujang came down from the tree, he was cruelly beaten with a bamboo cane, and his little stumpy tail was pulled until he shrieked with agony.

When they went to bed that night, Boon Ma whispered to Bujang:— "Little brother, it is no use. You are too small and weak. I could do it, but I am afraid. I am not brave like you. We must bear our hard lot, and make the best of things."

About a week later, by what may have been a strange coincidence, a similar accident occurred again. But this time, not only did the coconut fall in an outward direction from the tree, but it so happened that Lung Plien was standing unusually near to the trunk. Thus it came about that the heavy nut struck him squarely on the top of his head. As he was bald,

....it seemed to spring away in an outward direction and struck Lung Plien on the shoulder.

there was nothing to soften the blow. The old man fell prone at the foot of the tree, and died almost at once.

The cries of Boon Ma quickly attracted most of the neighbours to Lung Plien's garden. There they found the owner lying dead, Boon Ma vainly trying to revive him, and little Bujang gibbering and squealing aloft among the coconuts. Pu Tan related how he had seen a similar accident only a short time before. On that occasion, he said, Lung Plien had not been much hurt, but had accused the monkey of deliberately causing the coconut to strike him. He himself, however, was absolutely certain that such a thing was impossible. So everybody agreed that it was an unfortunate accident.

Lung Plien had no other relatives besides Boon Ma, who became the owner of the coconut garden, not to mention a considerable sum of money which the dead man was found to have in the bank. Pu Tan offered Boon Ma a home, so now the old man and the young lad are working their plantations together, and doing extremely well. Boon Ma attends the village school, and Bujang is well fed and cared for, and has quite forgotten what it feels like to be beaten or to have his ears and tail pulled.

But sometimes, when there is nobody near, Boon Ma whispers to Bujang:— "Tell me the real truth, little brother. Was it an accident, or did you give the coconut a shove?"

And little Bujang scratches himself and chuckles.

*   *   *

THE BREEDING PEARL

"A breeding pearl!" exclaimed Jim Peters.   "What on earth is the man talking about?"

Jim, a young Englishman of twenty-five, had just been appointed Assistant Manager of the Batu Puteh Tin Mining Company at Patani, and was on his way down to his new post by coasting steamer. He had gone ashore at Songkhla with the ship's Captain to have a look at the town, and they

172

had strolled into a shop where the Captain said there were pearls for sale. The old man who owned the shop had shown them a fair-sized pearl, and had asked a high price for it, on the ground that it was a breeding pearl.

"Why, don't you know," said Captain Jensen, "that almost all the people along the coast of the Malay peninsula believe in breeding pearls? They will tell you that if you put one of these pearls away, together with a little rice and some other necessary ingredients to nourish the pearl, such for instance as milk. and wait for a few months, a baby pearl will appear. I have heard it said so often that I have almost come to believe it."

"But the idea is ridiculous," exclaimed Jim; "a pearl is not a living thing. It is an inert lump of calcium covered with nacre. How can it possibly produce young ones?"

"My dear chap," answered Jensen, "there are a lot of queer things you will meet with round about these parts. Breeding pearls are accepted as quite a natural thing. Moreover, many people claim that you can make a pearl increase in size if you put it away and feed it properly. There was a lot of correspondence on this subject some time ago in the "Straits Sentinel." Quite a large number of Malays and Chinese wrote to claim that they had successfully bred baby pearls, or made pearls grow bigger by careful feeding. Moreover, a few Europeans wrote to say that they had enquired into this matter, and believed in the possibility of breeding pearls, or of increasing their size."

"Well," said Jim, "I think it is the most absurd thing I ever heard of in my life. Still, "when in Rome, do as the Romans do; I am coming to live in the Peninsula, so I too, will set up as a pearl breeder."

So, after a bit of hard bargaining, Jim bought the pearl for a fairly reasonable price, and he and the Captain went back to the ship.

*　　　*　　　*

After his arrival in Patani, Jim was for a time so busy absorbing the intricacies of tin mining that he forgot all about his pearl. Then, one morning, he came across the little box in which he had put the pearl, lying almost forgotten

173

at the bottom of his suit-case. At dinner that night, he asked his Manager, Tom Hamilton, with whom he shared a bungalow, whether he had ever heard of breeding pearls. Tom roared with laughter. "Of course I have heard of them," he said. "Everybody believes in them here. It is useless to argue with them about it. They will counter by pointing out that dogs and cats give birth to puppies and kittens; why, then, should not pearls have babies too? Moreover, they may mention that you have grown to your present hefty proportions because your parents brought you up on nourishing food. Why, therefore, should not a pearl grow bigger if properly fed?"

"Well," said Jim, "you may think me a fool, but I have actually bought a breeding pearl. Just for the fun of the thing, I will try to feed it up according to the local rules. and see whether it grows any bigger, or gives birth to any infants."

Tom once again laughed heartily. "If you want expert advice on pearl breeding and culture," said he, "you have got the very man you need right here in this bungalow. Your house-boy, Chalerm, told me some time ago that his father was a very successful pearl breeder. His family are Thai people who have lived in Patani for several generations, and are soaked up to the eyes in every sort of local superstition."

*　　　*　　　*

Jim lost no time in consulting his young servant Chalerm about his pearl. Chalerm accepted it as the most ordinary sort of matter. He examined Tom's pearl, and pronounced it to be a very good type of breeder. Then, under his servant's expert supervision, Tom put the pearl away in a pill-box. It lay on a little cushion of cotton-wool, and near it were placed a number of grains of rice, some lime, a slice of dried fish, and a small lump of wax. The important matter of a milk supply had then to be considered. Chalerm explained that success depended very largely on the use of a suitable type of milk. Cow's milk and goat's milk, he thought, were too strong. Horse's milk or human milk, he suggested, were better. As there was no horse's milk available anywhere near by, Tom decided on human milk. Luckily this was easy to

174

arrange. Chalerm's wife was actually suckling a baby at the time, and she willingly agreed to provide two or three drops of her milk twice a week to nourish the breeding pearl.

The extreme confidence shown by Chalerm in regard to his pearl and its breeding capacity came very near to awakening some degree of credulity in Jim's heart; but as the weeks passed by, and the pearl showed no change in size, and displayed no signs of pregnancy, he confessed to Tom Hamilton, who all along had treated the whole matter as a joke, that he had decided to send the pearl as a present to his sister, and not to bother himself any more about the matter.

However, just at this time, Jim was compelled to pay a visit to Bangkok to consult his dentist. Before he left, Chalerm begged him to leave the breeding pearl in his charge. To this he agreed, and while he was in Bangkok he almost forgot about the whole business.

*   *   *

When Jim returned to Patani, the first thing Chalerm did was to show him his pearl. To his surprise, he observed that it had distinctly increased in size. No doubt about it. The pearl had grown, and Chalerm assured his master that in a short time it was almost certain to give birth to a young pearl.

Tom Hamilton, as usual, was sceptical. "Chalerm is a young rascal," said he; "of course he has taken away your pearl and substituted a larger one."

But Jim would not agree to this. Why, he asked, should Chalerm steal a pearl in order to replace it by a larger and more valuable one? Obviously he would be the loser by any such action.

Another month passed by, the pearl had no babies, and grew no bigger. Then, one day, Jim went to visit a Chinese friend, Lim Yew Hok, who ran a large saw-mill some miles from Patani. Among his many labourers, Lim Yew Hok had one seldom seen in peninsular saw-mills, though common in Northern Thailand. This was a female elephant. Moreover, the saw-mill elephant was at that time suckling an elephant calf. A brilliant idea seized Jim Peters. He would ask his

Chinese friend for a small supply of elephant milk, and put it on his pearl. If elephant milk did not speedily produce several pearl babies, or increase the size of the breeding pearl to gigantic proportions, then nothing on earth would do so. Why not try?

Lim Yew Hok was quite willing to oblige, and Jim returned to Patani taking with him a small bottle filled with elephant milk which he carefully put in his refrigerator. Chalerm was very inquisitive concerning this bottle, but Jim refused to tell him anything. "I will show him," thought he, "that he is not the only man in the world who has original ideas about a suitable diet for breeding pearls."

Late that night, after Chalerm had gone home, and when Tom Hamilton was fast asleep, Jim got up, went to the refrigerator, got out the bottle of elephant milk, and let two drops if it fall upon his pearl.

*   *   *

Jim waited three days before going to have another look at the pearl, so as to give the elephant milk a fair chance to do its work. Then he opened the little box, half expecting to see therein either a whole brood of young pearls, or else a single pearl of enormous size. Alas! A tragic sight met his eyes. The pearl had vanished, and in the place where it had lain nothing was to be seen but a little heap of lime!

Jim called Chalerm, who burst into tears when he heard what had happened to the breeding pearl. "Some scoundrel murt have crept in and put some harmful substance onto our pearl," he wailed. "Who would do such a wicked thing? It is almost as bad as murder!"

Then Jim made full confession; he told his servant all about the elephant milk. Chalerm was plunged into despair. "Nai, Nai," he sobbed; "how could you have done such a rash thing as to put elephant milk onto our beloved pearl? Why did you not trust me? If you had done so, in the course of time we should have had dozens of baby pearls, and the mother pearl would probably have been one of the largest in the world. You could have sent it to your Queen, and she would have had it set in her crown, and would have made you a *Sir*, or even a *Lord*."

Tom Hamilton, sceptical as ever, had a full explanation ready. "Of course," said he, "Chalerm stole the original pearl and substituted a larger one. Then he seized the opportunity you gave him when you put elephant milk onto the new pearl, and stole that too, putting a little lime in its place, and pretending that the pearl had been disintegrated by the milk."

"But why should he do such a thing?" again asked Jim.

"Why, it's as clear as daylight," said Tom. "He stole the first pearl, then bought the larger one. Now he has taken that one too, and has got two pearls for the price of one. Moreover, no doubt he believes the first pearl to be a breeder. He is a Patani boy, born and bred here. He is certain to believe in breeding pearls. I have no doubt his father is now busily engaged in trying to raise a family out of your original pearl — but not using elephant milk!"

Jim, however could not bring himself, either then or later, to believe his servant capable of such frightful deceit.

Nevertheless, when Chalerm, a few weeks later, brought him another guaranteed super-quality breeding pearl, to be acquired at a rock-bottom price, Jim firmly withstood :emptation to buy it.